I0687404

His Family

by

Sheila Kell

HIS Series, Book Six

Cover Art by *Lea Schizas*

The Wild Rose Press, Inc.
PO Box 708
Adams Basin, NY 14410-0708
Visit us at www.thewildrosepress.com

Publishing History
First Edition, 2025
Trade Paperback Print ISBN 978-1-5092-5965-6
Digital ISBN 978-1-5092-5956-4

HIS Series, Book Six
Published in the United States of America

Dedication

In the loving memory of Amber Lauren Belle Howe
7-11-88 to 7-4-98
Her mother's "Angel Bunny"

Prologue

The crackling flames of the campfire had nearly died down when the real conversation began. Blake Hamilton's sons, along with foster son, Jake Cavanaugh, sat on the ground contemplating their futures without their big brother. With graduation from high school around the corner, Jesse had been accepted at the University of Maryland, and they were celebrating with a camping trip. It was only on the back of their Silver Spring, Maryland property, but they were alone. Or at least they thought they were.

Blake didn't mean to be a voyeur. He'd actually come looking for his daughter, Emily, who hadn't been happy her brothers got to camp out, and she wasn't permitted to join them. To her, there was no such thing as a "guys' night" for her brothers.

He'd spotted her behind some bushes with Trent McKenzie, the son he wished with all his heart he could claim publicly. But he'd made a deal with Trent's mother, which allowed him to see the boy grow up even though he had to keep silent about his origins. It constantly wrenched his heart out when his wife turned Trent away, increasing the suffering from his mistake. No. Not a mistake. Trent had never been a mistake.

The two were peeking in on the group of campers, so his interest had piqued as to what the topic happened to be and whether it would be deemed appropriate for her ears. The ones around the fire were healthy, good-looking, girl-chasing boys, after all.

But they weren't talking about girls—not at the moment, anyway. They were worried about what would happen when Jesse left. The truth was, they didn't need Jesse like when they were younger. When Blake had been too busy with his career to be the type of father they'd needed, Jesse had watched over his brothers.

It wrenched at his heart that Jesse took on the role. Blake should've been there more. He should've been the father they'd needed. Going through so many nannies should've clued him in they needed him when he'd been working to secure future elections for himself.

He'd made individual time for all his kids, but watching them, he realized it hadn't been enough. It might be too late to be that father to Jesse, but things would change before it was too late for his younger children.

Using a stick to draw in the dirt beside him, AJ wore his favorite Orioles T-shirt and sighed heavily. At ten years old, AJ was buddies with an eleven-year-old Jake. Because of when their birthdays fell, they were in the same grade, and when he'd enrolled Jake, he'd managed to get them in the same class.

As a hothead, AJ was apt to jump first and figure out he shouldn't have later. When he wasn't jumping into the fire, he believed the world was his playground. Maybe the family spoiled him too much. Whatever the case, Jake had a solid head on his shoulders and wouldn't allow AJ to lead them astray. "I thought we'd always be together."

Children usually believed that. The children had

thought that of their mother before she'd passed from cancer.

"We'll be together, just not living in the same house," Jesse said.

One of the twins snorted, and Jesse's head whipped toward them with a deadly gleam in his eyes. Brad and Matt, who'd just turned thirteen and sported black eyes, were still ornery and fighting over everything.

Blake shook his head at both the insolence of the snort and the stupidity of how they'd acquired those injuries. They'd broken each other's noses over a girl. At their age. So what that she'd kissed the both of them and then told each the other was a better kisser. They had to lighten up and stop being so randy if they were to survive high school girls.

As their father, he found the whole of the situation amusing—although he'd never admit it—but he'd also been resigned to how things could be until the two developed a thick skin so childish pranks by a mere slip of a girl wouldn't affect them.

Heaven help them all when the two are grown. One could hope that as they matured, so did their tastes, and in a different direction so they weren't both looking at the same girl.

"AJ, I need to go to college."

"But why?" his youngest son whined.

Seeming to try another tact, Jesse asked, "AJ, what do you want to be when you grow up?"

"A policeman." He straightened his shoulders with pride radiating from them. "But I'm going to live here," he hurriedly added.

"What about college?"

After AJ's inability to accept Jesse leaving for

college, Blake couldn't understand where his eldest son planned to lead this conversation.

Another sigh from AJ. "If I must."

The boy had no clue. Blake would have someone drag his ass to class every day in college if that was what it took for him to gain an education. As Jesse had found out, going to college—or not—wasn't negotiable in the Hamilton household.

"I'm going. If I can afford it." Jake pulled his knees close to his chest and rested his arms across them. His jeans looked as if they could be short. It was hard to tell since in that position anyone's pants would pull up that way. The boy was growing fast. "I hear there are ways."

Oh, he'd go to college and it'd be paid for but not from Jake's criminal father. Blake wouldn't allow Jake to be someone who fell through the cracks once he turned eighteen and foster care ended.

"What do you want to be, Jake?" Jesse asked.

"A policeman."

This, Blake knew. After having his father pulled off him by an officer, it had been a single focus of the kid.

"But I want college too," Jake added.

"I know." Eagerness flowed through AJ's words. "We can all be policemen together. Have our own unit at BPD. Dad could make it happen. I know he can."

Blake almost busted out laughing at that. The kid had a bit too much faith in his father, but if that was what they wanted, he'd work his ass off to make it happen. Anything for his kids.

Jesse shook his head. "It doesn't work like that. Besides, I think I'm going into the army after I graduate."

What the fuck? Blake's heart nearly stopped. This was news to him. He didn't know what to think. Pride. Fear. No, pride. His son knew what he wanted and was competent. Definitely pride. He only wished he'd been told first.

"What?" exploded from a sixteen-year-old Devon in a black T-shirt and jeans with holes in them. The boy was smart as a whip and could do almost anything with a computer. Blake saw MIT in his future and a recruiting call from either the CIA or NSA. From what Blake had heard from Jesse, instead of worrying about college and a future career, Devon was enjoying all the attention he received from the girls in high school.

Jesse picked up a wood chip and tossed it into the fire, watching it get devoured by the flames. "Yeah. I'll do ROTC and join. Hopefully one day they'll ask me to be a U.S. Army Ranger."

His pride in his son grew twofold.

"I want to be a SEAL."

Blake couldn't believe those words came from Matt. The young man, when not connected with Brad, was the opposite of what he expected of a SEAL. They were big, badass men who ate nails for breakfast. Matt was calm and peaceful. A hostage negotiator seemed more his speed.

"Like they'd take you," Brad taunted and leaned into Matt, shoving him with his elbow.

"What about you, Brad?" Jesse asked.

The teenager always tried to act big and bad around them, but Blake knew the real Brad, and he was gentle and kind.

Keeping the twins separated seemed key. When the

time came, he'd push for different colleges. That should do it since those years helped make a man. If they didn't beat the shit out of the other one before then.

"I'm going to be a bodyguard." He bowed up his scrawny chest wearing a shit-eating grin. "I'm going to protect hot movie stars and supermodels."

Everyone laughed. The kid did like to be comic relief.

"Why can't you all just be policemen with me and Jake?" AJ whined.

Blake wanted to go out there and soothe AJ and explain how they were all different, but he held his ground and left it to Jesse, since he wasn't supposed to be there.

"Well, because we all want different things," Jesse explained.

"But there has to be a place we can all work together," AJ insisted.

Brad stood. "We could all work for Dad," he turned and shot over his shoulder. Blake thought he'd been noticed. Instead, Brad took off in a different direction. "I gotta take a piss."

"I don't want to work for Dad. I want to wear a badge and protect people." AJ's voice took on that annoyed tone it did when he wasn't getting his way. Usually, they tried some way to please him.

In this, they couldn't help him because there was no way they could all work together. Even protecting people.

Just about to step away, thinking the conversation had ended, AJ jumped from his place. "I know. We can have our own company. Then we can work together."

Knowing this would go nowhere, he turned to

make his way to Emily and take her inside. As he neared them, his seven-year-old daughter told Trent, "I'm going to join them too."

"Aw, Em, they won't want a girl," said Trent in all his eleven-year-old wisdom.

She stuck out her chin in defiance and launched her hand on her hip, the tips of her fingers sliding under her pink top. "They will," she insisted. "I'll be Jake's wife, so they'll have to take me."

Jake's wife? What the fuck? He'd best watch those two.

Trent shook his head and rolled his eyes but said nothing to such a ludicrous statement.

That made him wonder what else he'd missed not being around much.

"And they'll take you too."

"I can't. I'm not a Hamilton."

If only he knew….

Grinning, Trent added, "And I'm not marrying Jake."

She scrunched up her mouth to show her displeasure. "Jake's not family either."

"True, but he's like family. Me? My mom works for your dad." He frowned. "I'm like the hired help."

That shot an arrow through his heart. He almost stepped out and broke the news, but at the last minute, he held back, keeping to his promise.

"I don't care, and neither will they," Emily insisted.

"Come on, let's go home before someone misses you." He reached out his hand, and she clasped her small one in his. So trusting.

Blake took an alternate trek back to the house to

avoid Emily and Trent. His mind spun the whole way. Wouldn't it be great if they all stayed together and owned a company? He couldn't be happier or prouder if that ever happened.

Chapter One

Seventeen years later

U.S. Senator Blake Hamilton always thought he'd be ready for anything that came his way. He'd once been a member of a black ops team, albeit short-lived. As a senator, he'd flown into dangerous territories where he had to wear a flak vest and helmet to greet troops. He'd faced down angry constituents who didn't agree with his stance. After his first few years in office, dealing with senior executive leadership was a cakewalk. Meeting with foreign leaders hadn't even thrown him off his game. He'd been raised as a senator's son, and he knew what it took to be a good senator, and he emulated it to the best of his ability.

Raising six boys and one girl—albeit with a host of nannies and other workers—had only added gray to his dark hair. Being a single father after their mother died had freaked him out initially, but the advice he'd received from his father guided him. *Handle everything with love and compassion.*

So, he had. And he'd handled everything else with the strength of his character and his resolve to be a good man.

Then came Elizabeth Page.

It'd been another fundraiser he'd agreed to attend with Drew, a fellow congressman. He was not paying much attention to the cause. He was just grateful he hadn't had to don his monkey suit. The tux got entirely too much wear as far as he was concerned. Instead, he'd worn his favorite Brioni dark gray suit, prepared to meet the woman who had Drew in knots.

As the evening had progressed, he'd learned the cause was Diamond Blackfan Anemia Awareness. It sickened him to hear of the destruction of this horrible disease. And while not widespread, it wasn't picky when it sought its victims.

After committing to a hefty donation, he turned his head to find this angel gliding toward him and Drew. Her long white gown shone as she passed the lights, glittering like pixie dust. With her blonde hair pulled up in some up-do thing women did, her long, slender neck called to his lips. His gut rotated into knots of desire. He had to meet this beautiful woman. Had to get to know her.

Reaching out her hands as she approached, she clasped both of Drew's outstretched hands and squeezed them.

"Senator Shelby, it's so great that you could come."

"I wouldn't miss a chance to see you, my lovely."

Shell-shocked, Blake stood there, trying to take in this lovely creature and…he couldn't even think of it without wanting to toss his cookies. This couldn't be who Drew had been raving about for weeks now. It couldn't. She had to be his.

"And"—she turned to Blake with a beautiful smile but still spoke to Drew—"who is this?"

That was a slap in the face. He'd been in politics for more than twenty years. He'd chaired more committees than he'd like to have done. His name and face were always plastered in the news. He was the fucking Senate minority leader.

Clearing his throat to speak for himself, he thrust out a hand to clasp hers. "I'm Blake Hamilton." Let her figure out if he was an important donor or not. If the name didn't knock sense into her, he had an uphill battle. At least from what he could tell from their initial interaction, she hadn't shown Drew any different emotions than she showed him.

"It's nice to meet you." She shook his hand with a soft one he could imagine running all over his body. "I'm Elizabeth Page." After dropping her hand, she waved it as if to encompass the area. "Thank you for attending tonight. I'll be glad to answer questions."

Although he'd learned plenty beforehand, he'd ask question after question to keep her close, to hear her voice, to catch a drift of her scent when he could. "What's the short overview of the disease?"

Her smile dimmed some with her response. "Diamond Blackfan Anemia is a disorder of the bone marrow. In Diamond Blackfan Anemia, the bone marrow malfunctions and fails to make enough red blood cells, which carry oxygen to the body's tissues."

"Is there a cure?"

Her smile disappeared altogether. "Sadly, no. Which is why foundations such as mine are so important. Building awareness and helping fund research are crucial in our attempts to beat this disease."

They spoke more in-depth about her foundation. With each fervent word she spoke, her passion for the project exploded to the surface as her face glowed and a light burned bright in her eyes. Her response stirred him and made him wonder if she'd be this passionate in bed.

Before that night, he hadn't been enjoying a robust sex life. Months ago, his latest mistress had wanted marriage, and he'd refused, so she'd walked. He imagined—knowing her—she expected him to come running back with his tail tucked between his legs when he realized how much he missed her. He only missed sex. She'd even taken the fun out of it until it was just plain old screwing.

He'd come to the realization that was all there was at his age. Hell, it wouldn't be much longer, and he'd have to have pills to get it up. At least that was what he'd been told. Right now, his dick worked fine. It just needed a good, warm place to park itself.

After the event, he'd gotten out of Drew that there wasn't a relationship between him and Elizabeth. Never before had he thought to put a woman over friendship, but with her, he would do it. He informed Drew that he planned to make a play for her. Laughing, his friend told him that she'd yet to choose anyone vying for her attention so Blake could waste his time beside him and others.

After years of working together, Drew should know that Blake didn't waste time, and he didn't lose.

****

It had taken a few months, but with a full-court press to gain Elizabeth's attention, he'd won. It hadn't been easy. She didn't play coy, but she hadn't wanted a relationship—with anyone. She'd been quite happy with her solitary life. But he hadn't given up, and finally, Elizabeth was his.

They'd been seeing each other ever since. They hadn't been a public couple, preferring to keep their relationship secret, but they'd been seen together at several events over the past year. A few people had figured out something was happening but preferred to speculate with their friends instead of asking.

And if they had asked, he'd have told them the truth—he'd fallen head over heels in love with her and planned to make her his wife. As far as he knew, she had no idea he was that serious about their relationship. Sure, they'd said they loved each other, but the heads-over-heels crap hadn't been discussed. He considered that the final level before taking the plunge—something he swore he'd never do again after his marriage to Camilla.

He wouldn't allow his mind to divert to his late wife. Marriage would work with Elizabeth. He just knew it. As for his kids, Elizabeth would be their stepmother, even though they were too old to have one, so he wanted their approval. Since he made all his calls and Facetime with his kids all about them, they hadn't met Elizabeth, and Blake hadn't spoken of her. Even if his children didn't approve—which he couldn't see how since she was absolutely perfect—he'd still propose, but he'd prefer their blessing.

So, he set up a family affair at their Oxford home to introduce Elizabeth to his children and grandchildren. Her future children and grandchildren by marriage. He'd have a day with her with no hectic social or work calendar to intrude, then the entire family was arriving. Then, proposing.

A knock sounded on the door to his study in his DC townhouse, effectively bringing his mind back to focus on his current task—get the hell out of here as quickly as possible and pick up Elizabeth.

"Come," he said more gruffly than he'd meant. It wasn't his assistant's fault he wanted to be gone.

Approaching the desk, Randy Rollins, the young kid he'd taken a chance on a few years ago, wore an uncommon frown.

Drawing his brows in, his gut clenching, Blake asked, "What's going on?"

Randy reached a shaky hand and slid a single sheet of paper onto Blake's desk. "They sent another one. I already called to have it traced, but it could be like the last couple and end up a dead end."

Blake reached across the desk, trepidation in his movement. With his fingers on the paper, Blake pulled it to him and read the same note they'd sent before. The same thing that confused the hell out of him.

Vote our way or you die.

How the hell did whoever sent this expect him to know which way to vote? On what? Not that he'd allow a threat to dictate that. But if they knew any of the Ws—who, what, why—they could stop the idiots sending these notes.

Death threats weren't uncommon, but the inability to track these brief messages told of someone a bit more intelligent than the average person who sends a threat. Yet, they've not said how to vote, so maybe they aren't all that brilliant after all.

With a heavy sigh that emptied his lungs, Blake leaned back in his office chair. "Maybe this time they screwed up."

"Do you think it's time to get some protection?"

Thinking for a moment, he shook his head. "No. It says if I don't vote, then I die. They obviously want me to vote on something, so it stands to reason they won't harm me." *Yet.* "I don't have anything to vote on until after I return from vacation. When I return, we'll reevaluate it then."

"Good luck with the proposal, sir." Randy nodded. "She'll say yes."

His gut clenched. He wouldn't accept any other answer from her but yes. Even if that meant kidnapping her and holding her hostage until it happened. Even though he joked, his gut clenched at the thought of something so terrible happening to her. No way would he hurt a hair on her precious head. God help the man who ever did.

Chapter Two

"I'm telling you, Beth, he's going to propose," Crystal said fervently.

Elizabeth Page gripped the phone and pushed it tighter to her ear. *If only he would.* "He'd best," she stated in response, even though one wasn't required. It generally wasn't with her friend who made bold statements without thinking them through before they left her mouth. "If not, I'll do it." She nodded even though Crystal couldn't see her. "We've been together more than long enough. Marriage is the next logical step." *And I want to marry Blake Hamilton with all my heart.*

A gasp sounded on the other line. "You wouldn't."

Standing straighter, Elizabeth jutted her chin out and huffed a little breath in commitment. Yes, she would. In a heartbeat. In fact, she probably should've done it to move things along with the two of them. Lord knew he was taking his sweet time. "I'm tired of never being able to spend our full nights together or touching in public because he's worried about my reputation and how it would impact my foundation." Before Blake, her foundation had been everything to her. It was her only link to her daughter. Now, he took a slice of that everything pie. And she wouldn't give up either him or the foundation or knowingly do damage to either.

Exhaling a long sigh, her shoulders relaxed from

their tense stance. He'd been right in his beliefs—as old-fashioned as they sounded. People might misconstrue their relationship and call her playing the whore for donations since he'd made a very substantial one and invited his friends to events and helped solicit contributions.

But oh, she wanted it all. The happy ending she knew only he could provide. She'd loved her dearly departed husband, but not with the ferocity of her love for Blake. Or the passion. That sweet passion where they almost ignited being near each other.

Blake Hamilton represented everything good in men and politics. Always voting with his conscience and not just with his party earned him a great deal of grief from time to time, but he was able to sleep at night by voting for what was right. And when he was passionate about something, he'd stop at nothing to get his message out and sway those he needed to win his vote. He worked for the people, not a party.

He also still opened doors for her and carried her bags, all the stuff gentlemen of old used to do. The things you didn't see anymore, mostly due to the lack of common courtesy demonstrated more often today. Sure, she could do her own things, and would, but if he offered, it didn't offend her—it endeared him to her.

Heck, add a few flashy weapons on him, and he'd be Captain America in her mind.

That image did generate a chuckle from her that Crystal ignored as she kept rambling. Thank goodness because she'd hate to explain that image to her friend.

"But that's a good thing he's done that. Now he's taking you away for a long weekend, and you're meeting his children. He's going to propose," Crystal reiterated with just as much passion as the first time.

Laughing, Elizabeth turned the call on speakerphone. She set it down on the bed beside her suitcase so she could pack while talking. Picking up a cream blouse, she folded it while she got her laughter under control. "You sound like a broken record." After placing the blouse in her suitcase, she picked up a pair of navy slacks and proceeded to fold them. She knew she was overpacking, but she had no idea what to expect, except heat and humidity. A shudder spiraled up her spine at what occurred when she met the two elements. She pictured everything sticking to her, soaking wet, and her hair plastered to her head. Blake said it wasn't that bad in August, but he was used to it and probably didn't realize how bad it truly was for someone who didn't live or frequent Mississippi.

"What kind of ring do you think he's purchased? Princess? Diamond cut? Ooh, maybe an emerald surrounded by diamonds."

Elizabeth shook her head. She'd had enough of the conversation. Instead of getting her hopes up, she should practice how she'd propose to him. She could do it. Okay, she might be a smidge nervous…maybe a bit cowardly on the idea, but she had to have a game plan.

One thing was for certain, she had to win over his children. When they'd discussed keeping their relationship secret, she and Blake had agreed not to tell his children, which could've been his simple code for "I don't want my kids bugging me about us whenever we talk." She just went with it since it was his family.

Blake's children were about all that he spoke about. His love for them was monumental. If only she could grasp a slice of it, then life would be perfect.

Her spine snapped straight. What if his kids didn't like her and that meant he wouldn't propose? With a sinking heart, she turned over the idea in her mind. Something within told her Blake was his own man and his children were grown. Nothing would stop him if that was what he wanted. But did he want it?

The doorbell interrupted her response to Crystal. "Hold on a second. Someone's here."

"Who?" Crystal asked in a serious tone.

That was a good question. She checked her watch to make sure it wasn't Blake's driver picking her up. No, she had plenty of time. Plenty of time provided this wasn't a visitor who expected to be entertained.

Out of habit, she picked up her phone and then walked to the front door. Peeking outside, she saw a deliveryman, but he didn't have the flowers Blake typically sent her. Then again, it wouldn't make sense for him to send flowers today since she wouldn't return until they were dead or close to it.

Easing the door open, with the cell phone in her hand at her side, she smiled when she saw the heavyset man holding a gift basket in his hands.

"Delivery for Elizabeth Page," he said in a bored voice.

Wow. He definitely didn't care about tips with that attitude. She always believed in giving them something, though. Since Blake had taken to sending her flowers regularly, she'd stashed away some ones and fives in a little container on a small table near the front door so she didn't have to search out her purse each time.

"I'm Elizabeth," she finally said with her interest piqued at the contents of the basket.

The man extended the basket, and she grabbed it

by the handle. Not too heavy, but it appeared full of stuff. She saw a travel pillow and smiled. Curiosity flowed through her at what else the man she loved had put together for her.

"Hold on a moment." She stepped back and set the basket on the floor right inside her home, dropped the phone on the table, and reached for her container. After grabbing a few bills, she turned back and extended them to the deliveryman. "Thank you."

He nodded and walked away. *Grouch.* Then she almost snickered out loud at that thought.

After closing the door, Crystal shouted from the phone she'd forgotten on the small table. "Who was it? It sounded like a delivery. Did you get more roses?"

With a little pep in her step, she picked up the phone and the basket and moved swiftly to her bedroom. "It's a basket. I don't know what's all in it yet. Give me a minute."

"Is it from Blake? Never mind, stupid question. Of course it's from Blake. The man should just employ his own deliveryman."

Laughing, she set the phone down on the bed, then flipped the lid of the suitcase closed to make room for the basket. Once on the bed, she untied the top and opened the cellophane wrap. She covered her mouth with a gasp and then a big smile split her face. He remembered.

"What is it?" her friend persisted in asking.

Giggling, she said, "It's a travel basket. He remembered I get motion sickness sometimes."

"So what—he sent you motion sickness pills?"

She nodded, then remembered Crystal couldn't see her. "Among other things." She began emptying the basket. "A travel pillow to sleep on the plane. Motion sickness pills tied to a travel blanket. A small size of peach antibacterial lotion. Peach lip balm. A bag of cashews. A bag of dried peaches. And a dark chocolate bar."

The thought that went into the basket overwhelmed her. She dropped on the small space open on the bed. He'd truly listened to her and what she liked. He'd asked once and remembered.

"Wow, Beth, that's…amazing." The awe in her friend's voice matched the awe inside her.

"I know."

"Does it have a note?"

Elizabeth started at that. She'd seen one but had been too excited about the items. "Hang on." Reaching into the basket, she noticed her hand trembling as she retrieved the note.

My love,

My arms are always there for you, but I thought these items might bring you comfort during our travels.

B.

She read the letter to her friend.

"Yep, he's going to propose," Crystal said before Elizabeth had finished saying the letter B.

"How do you get it from this note? There's nothing special in there to allude to that." Elizabeth read it again and love rolled through her veins. She'd found the most wonderful man alive, and she wasn't going to let him get out of her grasp.

"Just trust me."

Knowing the conversation would go nowhere else and the fact she had to pack, she decided to end her call with her friend. "I need to get packing. Goodbye,

Crystal."

"Okay, have a good trip and call me as soon as he proposes."

She shook her head. "Bye."

So he might propose, but he might not. At this point, she didn't care. No way would she allow that man to get loose of her grasp. She wanted a full life with him. To be his wife. To be in his bed every night. Yep, there was nothing else to do. She'd have to propose to him.

Chapter Three

Every time he rode up to the house in Oxford, his heart swelled with joy at all the memories of vacations spent here with the kids. If he'd allowed, Camilla would've moved her and the kids here while he tirelessly worked in D.C.

Lacking normal family vacations, he'd spent most of his time here to attend Ole Miss sports events. With him attending there and then his twin sons—Brad and Matt—doing the same, the house was lively every game weekend. And in Oxford, during game weekend, having a guaranteed place to stay during that time was a must.

But he wasn't selfish.

This home belonged to the entire family whenever they wanted to get away from it all. Some had vacationed with friends, and it pleased the hell out of Mary, their housekeeper, to have them come back to visit. She hadn't been there when the kids had been small, but they'd been small enough in her eyes for her to adopt them as her own.

As for the house, heck, his sons, who owned Hamilton Investigation & Security, had used it as a safe house before when they'd been protecting clients. Pride radiated through him at all his sons had accomplished. Although now he shouldn't say sons since his daughter Emily had joined them at HIS, as they were more commonly called. And Jesse had nothing but high praise for her abilities. In fact, once, they'd hidden her and his granddaughter Amber here when someone was after them.

His heart nearly stilled thinking about that trip when things had gone horribly wrong. But he wouldn't go there now. This was a happy time.

"Oh my," Elizabeth said beside him. "It's lovely. I love the wraparound porch with all the azalea bushes."

The yellow, wooden two-story home had been a favorite of the entire family. With the guest house, he could just squeeze in the group this time, provided the younger girls slept together in one room and the twins still bunked in the same room. That was how they'd sleep on this trip once they arrived. He hoped Mary had the place ready for the bunch. Hell, he probably should've told her to hire some help, although he imagined his daughters-in-law wouldn't take to being pampered in a family home.

Driving his rental car past the oak- and magnolia-lined drive, he thought about the purpose of the trip. He'd never been so nervous in his life. There'd been no indication from Elizabeth that they should move to the next step. Doubt crept into his mind, but he shoved it aside. He wanted this, and he could only try.

First, he had two tasks to accomplish, and he didn't relish doing either. Elizabeth had to know the truth about what happened in his first marriage and what he'd done. He had to assure her that he'd be true, even though his track record dictated otherwise. Second, he wanted to tell his children first that he planned to ask her to marry him. While he didn't need to garner their approval, he hoped for it. They'd never know the truth about his marriage to their mother because he'd never tarnish her memory in their eyes, but he deserved someone who loved him for him, not for his position or what could be in the future.

As always, Mary and Henry Jones waited on the doorstep. Finding the right couple to trust to live in the house year-round had been a challenge. When an old friend of his said he was selling his home and didn't know what to do about his live-in housekeeper and handyman, Blake had hired them on the spot after hearing great things about the couple over the years. While in their early sixties, the two still got around like spring chickens. Blake had given them free rein to hire more help anytime the family was in residence or a big job needed to be done, but they rarely did it. He figured they didn't want to feel they couldn't do the job.

When it did become too taxing on their bodies and minds, he'd retire them and move them to the guest cottage to live out their remaining years if they chose. With several children living around the world, he had no idea if they'd accept the offer or if they'd visit their children and grandchildren. Heck, they could have great-grandchildren by then.

After exiting the vehicle, he stretched his arms up and leaned back, his muscles thanking him for the relief of the travel-weary strain. He may still work out when he was able, and ate right, but his body wasn't twenty years old any longer. He sometimes had a hard time remembering that.

Walking around to the trunk to retrieve the luggage, he inhaled the fresh air and the sweet scent of the many azalea bushes lining the front yard. There were a host of other smell-good plants, but he had no idea what they were called and didn't even try to figure them out or ask.

Funny, he never noticed how polluted the air was in D.C. until he came back here to visit. Out of sight, out of mind.

Elizabeth joined him. "Thank you for bringing me here."

He stopped retrieving the luggage and turned to her. His chest tightened, her beauty taking his breath away. Wearing her hair down for a change, with it hanging straight and dropping a few inches below her shoulders, she looked so much younger than her forty-seven years. With her hazel eyes looking at him with joy, his heart swelled with love. Lifting a hand, he settled it behind her head just above the nape of her neck.

He had to taste her sweet lips. It had been a long day of travel since their direct flight had been canceled. They'd eventually found one but had to make a connection in Atlanta.

As if sensing what was about to happen, Elizabeth pulled back hesitantly and with a right to do so. He'd never kissed her publicly before. They'd never let the proverbial cat out of the bag on their relationship. But that damn cat was getting kicked to the curb after this weekend.

Sensing her confusion, he smiled and winked at her. She scrunched up her face a moment as if trying to determine his game. In the end, she smiled back and relaxed into his hold.

The closer he got to her lips, the greater his anticipation. In truth, he wanted to grab her and carry her to the room and have his way with her, but he settled for a tender kiss that didn't even come close to satisfying his craving for her.

Elizabeth didn't have the same resolve as he did to keep it light. She kissed him again, her lips soft and warm over his, and her tongue licking the seam of his lips, seeking entrance.

How could he—a healthy, red-blooded man—deny her this?

With his hand, he adjusted the angle of her head and joined her in the embrace. Opening his mouth, his tongue darted out to slip past her open wet lips. Their tongues met and danced with an erotic movement that sent blood rushing to his groin.

Unable to resist the temptation that was Elizabeth, the kiss turned hungry, and when he passed the point of a semi-erection, he knew he had to quit because he didn't want to greet the hired help with a raging hard-on. They'd speculate enough over what his bringing her here meant.

Breaking apart from the love of his life was harder than he'd thought. But with an iron will, he did it. Seeing her cheeks flushed red with desire made him want to kiss her all over again.

"We, um—" He cleared his throat from the raspiness that had invaded his voice. "We'd best stop now or we'll end up giving a show to Mr. and Mrs. Jones, and I'm not sure their hearts are up for it." He grinned, his heart expanding at her laughter.

They unloaded and each rolled a bag. Craving her touch, he reached out and did something else he hadn't done before in public—he held her hand. It felt liberating to finally have their relationship out in the open.

He could only hope she didn't shut the door on

them permanently after he told her everything.

It had to happen tonight, or he'd not rest the entire trip.

****

"That was an incredible dinner." Standing on the porch beside Blake, Elizabeth held a hand to her flat stomach. "Mary is an amazing cook. I'm surprised no one has stolen her from you."

Blake flashed what had been called his one-thousand-watt smile and winked. "I'm one hell of a boss."

Laughing, Elizabeth's face brightened, reminding him of sunshine. "I have to wonder." She tapped a finger to her chin and grinned mischievously. "You're an absentee boss…so is it you as the boss or you not being present they enjoy most?"

"Ha ha ha," he said jovially, loving her joking nature. He placed his finger over his heart and pleaded, "How can someone not love me?"

She burst out laughing. "You're right. And I do love you."

Would she still say that when she learned he'd once tossed aside his vows? "I love you, too."

When she turned to him, his heart almost seized at the seriousness of her expression. Had he asked his question out loud?

"Will you tell me about your children again?" she asked softly. "I'll admit that I'm nervous meeting them, and I don't want to get them all mixed up. There seems to be so many with wives, a husband, and children in the mix."

He wrapped his arm around her and pulled her close. "They'll love you and not only because I do, but because you're an amazing and lovable woman." He prayed they did because he'd hate to see a break in his household. He wouldn't give her up or stop being in his children's lives.

This time, he planned to tell her about his first marriage. She'd never asked about his or he about hers, but he had to tell her and assure her that he would always be true to her. Yes, he'd have to tell her the entire dirty truth. Something he'd kept locked away since the day he was forced to propose to Camilla Rose.

Putting his hand behind her back, he gently pushed her forward. "Come on. I've got a great place for us to watch the sunset." But he'd tell her before it got dark, so he could see her true emotions on the subject of his past and their future.

She hesitated, then she moved forward. "And you'll tell me about them?"

With a firm nod, he continued urging her forward. "I'll tell you all about them."

Seemingly satisfied, she smiled and picked up her step around the patio. Taking three steps down, they landed on a narrow, pebbled path lined with rose bushes of many shades, and continued walking, single file, with Elizabeth in front of Blake. The crunching sound of their steps on the rocks sounded as they made their way to the end of the path and a small sitting area that held several white Adirondack chairs in a circle around a large, round, low-to-the-ground coffee table in a brushed-bronze frame.

Over the fragrance of the roses, the scent of recently cut grass still filled the air, and Blake relaxed as the welcome smell filled his nostrils. There was something about fresh-cut grass that rejuvenated him.

Henry knew that when Blake visited, he sometimes enjoyed riding the powerful mower around the lawn, gathering his thoughts and clearing his mind all at the same time. Knowing he'd accomplished something constructive while he'd done just that—and seen the fruits of that labor—made sitting there on the piece of lawn equipment worthwhile in his mind. This time, however, Henry had cut the grass in anticipation of Blake and Elizabeth's visit.

Curious, he wondered if the handyman knew he wanted to impress Elizabeth. Although when she became his wife, this estate would not belong to them. It'd been Camilla's dowry when they'd wed so long ago. He'd had no idea they still did that crap in modern days, but rich people could sometimes do weird things. He'd only kept it at this point so the entire family would have a retreat whenever they wanted. In the end, the estate would go to Emily. Their only daughter.

That had been one of the agreements he'd made on Camilla's deathbed. The other had been wrong of her to ask, but he'd agreed. He'd kept the one not to remarry while the kids were old enough to call someone else Mom. The thought of depriving the children of a mother figure had nearly killed him, but he hadn't found anyone he'd wanted to marry—until now.

Thinking of that made him realize that tonight he would come clean. So he'd worked to set the stage nicely. Mary would bring out a tray of refreshments after they settled in their chairs. Then she'd disappear.

Elizabeth looked back over her shoulder and slowed her pace. "I feel it trying to cool down already."

Although it was August, the weather had cooled enough that one could sit outside without sweating to death.

It being late evening, the blood-sucking mosquitoes could pose a problem soon. Thankfully, Henry had set out and lit citronella candles on the center table and a few small side tables to help with that problem.

Blake guided her to a chair facing away from the house. From there, she had a view of the lush expanse of green lawn before them. A perfect line of sight to watch the sun descend and change the sky to night.

"This is wonderful, Blake."

After sitting in a chair beside her, he smiled. "It's a great place to end the day."

"Are you going to tell me about your children? The way you keep putting it off is making me worry. Do you think they won't like me?"

"There is no doubt in my mind that they'll love you."

"Good. Then tell me. I remember their names. I think."

Damn, she was a persistent thing. "I am going to tell you, but I must tell you the story of my first marriage so you will understand about Trent."

"Trent?" She scrunched up her face, then shook her head. "I don't remember his name."

He reached over and threaded his fingers through hers on the arm of her chair. "That's because I haven't said anything about him. Just do me a favor and listen before you judge."

Nervousness laced her voice when she spoke. "Blake, what's going on? You don't have to tell me about your first marriage. That's in the past."

Tightening his grip on her hand, he pulled his lips into a grim line. "But your understanding of my past is critical."

Her brows dipped. "But why?"

"Just listen, okay?" he pleaded softly.

She visibly swallowed. "I'll listen, but you're scaring me, Blake."

"There's nothing to be scared of." He tilted his head. "That's not true. It's scary for me, because I need for you to know things are different with us."

Chapter Four

Trembling inside, Elizabeth allowed Blake to continue holding her hand while he spoke. She didn't understand why he wanted to talk about his first marriage. Lord knew she didn't want to talk about hers. They didn't matter to the now and the future. Unless he was going to tell her he was still married, she didn't care.

Yet talking of his marriage visibly bothered him, so she'd listen and hope no secret came out that had her wanting to run for the hills. Although there were no hills around here, just a bunch of magnolia trees.

"I was a senator's son with promise. I'd interned at the White House while in college. I went to Ole Miss and met Camilla, a local girl who I kept running into at social functions." He raised his eyebrows. "Elite social functions." Shrugging, he continued, "We hit it off nicely and started dating. I thought she cared for me, but I learned—too late—" he said bitterly, "that she cared for her future and that alone."

Sensing his upset, she offered, "Blake, you don't have to do this."

He squeezed her hand. "Yes, I do. There's something important in here, and I want you to know the why."

Not understanding but nodding, she smiled as best she could, considering she worried about what he planned to reveal.

"Camilla and I didn't love each other. Not in the way married people should. Oh, in the beginning she may have loved me like that, or maybe it was just the idea of what I'd become. Anyhow, right out of college, she told me she was pregnant. I was stupid enough and took her word for it. We rushed and got married. Turns out," he spat, "she wasn't pregnant." His voice turned hard as he continued. "She just wanted to ride my coattails. As a senator's son, I had a lot of promise in her eyes and her mother had raised her to be a socialite—to marry well. Knowing her mom and the viper she was, it's possible Camilla targeted me." He shrugged a shoulder. "But I didn't know for sure nor did I ask."

Her heart broke for him. To be lied to and treated as such. All because of who he was. She prayed he didn't think that of her. Oh no, was that why he was telling her? Was he testing her? Before she could put something from her thoughts into words, he continued.

"When we'd married, I'd been ecstatic about being a father. I spoiled her, and we made plans. Big plans. Once I found out she'd lied, our marriage took a turn for the worse. She knew I couldn't divorce if I wanted my political career to be without any dirty secrets. My father had agreed to that and recommended I try to work it out. That's when I realized he was in a loveless marriage himself. I'd never noticed it before, but it was then I saw they didn't touch or look at each other unless it was for a career purpose. I didn't want that for myself, so I vowed I'd love her no matter that she'd lied."

Being daring, Elizabeth stood and went to Blake,

smiling before she slid onto his lap. He put his arms around her and hugged her tightly. When she leaned her face down to his, he greedily attacked her mouth.

After kissing her breathlessly, he broke off and touched a finger to her cheek, sliding it down and sending a delicious shiver traveling through her.

He dropped his hand and settled it on her thigh. Looking out over the landscape, he grimaced. "Instead of going straight into a political career, I joined the Marines. It, of course, didn't go over well. We had Jesse and Devon. When she had the twins, I called it quits and tried to follow the path my family had created for me. I won a senate seat, and we'd developed an easy camaraderie between us. It wasn't love, but it worked. Then I caught her cheating. It was like I'd been gut-shot. I'd worked so hard to live this life, and she hadn't cared enough. She'd always coerced me into things for the betterment of my career. What she did could have destroyed it."

Running her fingers through his hair, she sighed. "Oh, Blake. That's terrible. You deserved better."

"Believe it not, she tossed me out and threatened divorce and telling everyone I'd cheated all over the place. At that point, I hadn't cared about my career. I'd been elected, and getting reelected was much easier since I had a good record. Then she did the unthinkable; she threatened to keep the kids from me. I was devastated.

"I moved into the little townhouse I had in D.C. instead of just staying there when I was in town. I didn't know what to do. I tried to get her to let me move back into our home. Try to work things out, but she was in love with the man she'd been cheating on me with.

Or so she said."

How could anyone be so cruel to this wonderful man? And to try to keep him from his children. What a bitch. Of course, she wouldn't say that to him, or his children, whom she guessed didn't know this about their mother. Thank God Blake was such an honorable man.

"Here's where things take a turn. Over the course of the years, I'd developed an attraction to my assistant. I hadn't acted on it because it wouldn't have been right, but after that betrayal and threat, and the possible loss of everything I held dear, I found myself in her arms."

Elizabeth couldn't contain her gasp.

"Lily was sweet and everything Camilla wasn't. We had a brief, very brief, affair while Camilla did her ranting and raving. Lily was the one who convinced me that I had to work things out with my wife, for the kids' sake. So, I did. I got dirty and discredited the man Camilla planned to take up house with so that she wouldn't have her socialite status like she had with me."

He shook his head. "It was wrong, but it got me my children back, so I won't feel bad about it. I didn't lie, only allowed the truth of his true business dealings to come to light."

"There's nothing wrong with that, Blake. Especially if she planned to make that man your children's stepfather. He needed to be removed from the picture if he was dirty."

"Yeah, well, imagine my surprise when not even a week later, Lily came to me and told me she was pregnant. She thought I should know but also that she'd keep it quiet because she didn't want to hurt my career.

No one would ever know she carried my child, including the child.

"I didn't know how I felt about that, but she was adamant that if I didn't agree, she'd disappear. So we compromised, and she moved into a cottage on the estate, much to my wife's spitting and fighting. Not long afterward, Roger McKenzie came from Lily's past, and they got married."

She wanted to say "Oh, Blake" again, but felt she should be saying something else. Yet she also needed to process this. He cheated on his wife—while they were separated—and had an illegitimate child he wouldn't acknowledge. How did she feel about it all?

He broke his vows no matter what happened. If things got rough with them, would he fall into another woman's arms? How could she trust him? Internally, she sighed. She just had to trust him. She couldn't imagine him ever being in the same position because she wouldn't cheat on him or kick him out, and she couldn't refuse to let him see his children. They were grown men and a woman.

"I kept my promise, but it killed me. With Lily living on the property, at least I got to watch Trent grow up with the others, even if it was from an outsider's perspective most of the time."

So that was why she needed to learn about Trent. Hopefully, he grew up with a loving father since Blake couldn't be one for him.

"When I had a heart attack, I knew I couldn't go to my grave without acknowledging him. I didn't give a shit what it did to my political career. Since his mother was dead, I felt it okay to tell him." He paused. Tears glimmered in his eyes. "He didn't think so."

Her heart broke for him and all that he'd lost. Leaning down, she hugged him. "Oh, Blake." So she'd said it again. It was needed. She gave him a quick kiss on the lips before sitting back up and letting him continue.

"Then," he said, choking up, "he could've died from a bomb blast saving my granddaughter—his niece. And he still wouldn't see me."

Sadness seeped into her at what darkness must've been there when Blake had been denied again and at such a critical point. She stroked his neck while she reached for his hand with her other one and threaded her fingers in his and squeezed.

"Trent took off after that for a few months, and while my kids didn't admit it, I think they knew where he was. I don't know exactly what happened to change his mind, but a few months ago he spoke with me and offered to give it a try. Not to be a replacement father, but to get to know each other better. We've talked some since then, but not nearly what I'd like. I may never get that though."

"Is he coming with the others?" she asked softly, knowing this could mean the world to Blake.

"I'm not certain. He never said one way or another. They have a two-month-old—Ashley—so I imagine he was waiting to see how she and her mother, Kelly, are feeling."

"Maybe we'll be lucky and see them this trip."

Blake toyed with her hand laced with his. "You're not—I mean—" He cleared his throat. "Hell, I don't know what I mean. I just told you I cheated during my first marriage."

How could her heart not expand with love for this

man? She couldn't condone the cheating, but she believed he didn't seek it out. Didn't try to be a philanderer. "You did. That's the past."

"Aren't you worried if we get married that I might cheat on you?"

Her pulse rate sped up. Was he about to ask her to marry him? Right now? "Well, um, I trust you." There, she'd said it and that would be her mantra. She had no reason to distrust him since he loved her, unlike his first wife.

He reached behind her neck and slowly drew her down to him. "You are an amazing woman, Elizabeth Page." Then he kissed her and made her forget everything, including to breathe.

Chapter Five

How did he get so damn lucky to find a woman who would not hold his past against him? Who would love and trust him as he was? Blake worried himself to a near ulcer that she'd turn him away when she found out. Faithfulness in a marriage was expected, and he'd tossed it to the wind. He couldn't excuse himself because it was his dick that was used to cheat.

Had he not had the boys—Jesse, Devon, Brad, and Matt—he might've weathered the divorce storm in his career. Lord knows he'd been much happier with Lily.

Yet he still hadn't held the power of love...the depth of it that he carried for Elizabeth. He had no idea why it had taken him so long to find the love of his life, but he wasn't about to let her go anywhere. As soon as she met the children, he would propose. They'd love her. How could they not?

She was so perfect—beautiful, kind, caring, and so much more—that he wondered how she'd stayed single after the death of her husband so many years ago.

He'd like to believe she was waiting for him. He was tired of ensuring her reputation stayed pristine for the benefit of her foundation. Waking up at night alone sucked balls, and he planned to remedy that. This weekend was the start of a lifetime of waking with her beside him.

Slowly chewing the last bite of the Boston creme

pie Mary made for them, he washed it down with iced tea. He turned to watch Elizabeth wrap her mouth around a forkful of pie. When she closed her eyes and sighed in pleasure, his dick came to life, imagining her lovely mouth encircling his growing erection.

Damn.

After she had put her fork down, he reached over. "Here," he said softly as he placed a piece of pie on the fork, "let me."

Their eyes locked and heat flamed in hers that he guessed matched his own. Holding the fork to her lips, he offered, "Take a bite."

With a smile, she opened her mouth and closed her lips over the pie. He groaned with his nearly painful need for her. "Are you full?" he croaked. The meal earlier had kept them both satisfied until they'd decided to enjoy this late-night treat. With the unknowing way Elizabeth erotically ate it, he'd have one made for her every fucking night.

"Yes," she said softly and reached for her dishes.

He did the same, and they deposited them in the sink as Mary had instructed. She'd probably flip her lid if after sending them away for the evening, he did her work.

"Where is Mary?" She looked around as if expecting the woman to appear out of thin air.

He sidled up next to her then put his arms around her, pulling her close. "They're visiting their daughter. We have the house to ourselves all night," he whispered near her ear.

She shivered, and he smiled because he knew that she felt it too—that magnetic draw between them that set their bodies alight. The pull that had hit him the first moment he'd seen her at the party.

Inhaling what he'd come to learn was her peach-scented lotion, he alternately kissed and nibbled a path down her neck. Midway in his trek, he took a shaky breath and asked, "Are you ready to go upstairs?" His dick strained against his zipper, and he feared it would either burst out or have a permanent zipper imprint on it. Either way wasn't how he planned his dick's entrance into their lovemaking tonight.

With a breathy sigh, she nodded and arched her neck to give him better access.

He looked at the creamy expanse of her throat and wanted nothing more than to cover the entire area with his lips, showing her how much he loved her and her body. But it took all his will to stop—to say wait until they got to the room. Otherwise, he'd be christening the counter. She deserved better than that. However, the idea had merit. He mentally shook his head. No. The bed.

Stepping back, he held out his hand to her as he always did when they went to bed. The difference was this time, they'd wake together. The thought was heady, and he couldn't wait until dawn and her smiling face being the first he saw when he opened his eyes.

Smiling, she clasped her hand in his and squeezed. "Let's go to bed."

She sounded calmer than he had. They walked through the kitchen to the stairway, which had the living room on the other side. He would miss this house, but it was time to turn it over. Hopefully he'd still have a room to visit and go to Ole Miss games.

Elizabeth rubbed her hands on the polished mahogany banister. "I love this house."

His heart sank like a rock in a lake. "It's not really mine."

Drawing in her brows, she looked at him in confusion.

They stopped their progress on the stairs. "I mean, I've kept it as if it were mine, but it's not. In fact, I decided it's time to give it to my daughter. That's what her mother wanted, and this was Camilla's house." *Please don't let that disappoint her and make her want to pull away.*

"Well, your daughter is lucky you did such a wonderful thing for her."

"You're not—disappointed?"

She leaned toward him, and he wanted to slip in and kiss her luscious lips. "I love you, Blake Hamilton. Not who you are or what you have. You." Placing her lips on his, she slid her free hand around the back of his neck.

His dick turned to stone. Her sweet taste intoxicated him. As his tongue swept into her mouth, he knew he couldn't get enough. He was also aware the stairs were not the place to get even more hot and bothered.

Breaking the kiss, he fought for breath in his air-deprived lungs. Damn. The effect the woman had on him was positively electrifying. "Come on." He tugged on her hand and continued up the stairs. At the door at the end of the hallway, he pushed it open and preceded her inside.

Mary had tidied up from where they'd haphazardly tossed their luggage after emptying it. The covers, white sheets with a blue comforter, were turned down, and a peach rose lay on the side where Elizabeth would sleep. Originally from Georgia, everything was peach for the woman—food, lotion, decorations, candles. He mentally snapped his fingers. He'd forgotten to have peach candles for Elizabeth's visit.

Seeing three large candles on the dresser, he walked to them and, with the lighter lying beside them, he lit them and caught a whiff of light, pleasant scent. It would do.

Elizabeth walked up beside him and removed her shoes. She dropped down the inch or so her heels had been on the shoes. "That smells good."

Sporting a wicked smile, he leaned into her and whispered, "You smell good."

When she leaned her neck for him, he went back to attacking it. Between nips, he commanded, "I want to undress you so don't even start."

On a breathy sigh, she dropped the hands that had been tugging her blouse up and over her head. "Hurry, then."

Although he didn't wish to rush, urgency drove him. Replacing her hands on her soft blouse, he pulled it up. He leaned back and watched as he exposed her lacy peach bra. A smile split his face. He should've known it'd be peach. And he bet her underwear matched. They always did.

Impatient, she raised her arms for him to dispose of her blouse and move on to her other clothing.

Appeasing her, he hurried to remove her blouse and slacks. Then he stood back again and drank in her beauty. It wasn't enough. He wanted her completely naked.

When she reached back to unclasp her bra and allowed it to slide down her arms and flutter to the floor, he remained rooted to the spot with his dick throbbing painfully. Her placing her fingers into the waistband of her panties almost sent him over the edge at the sight of her body bare to him. He ripped at his clothes and somehow managed to free himself without ruining them, not that he would have cared at this point. He just wanted to be inside Elizabeth's heat where he could lose himself in her.

Buck naked, his dick pointing up, he strolled to her naked form and quickly pulled her body to his. "You're so damn beautiful." Then he feasted on her scrumptious lips. She didn't fight it; in fact, her tongue darted out first, seeking his. They tangled, they played, he sucked the tip of her tongue in his mouth. He mimicked what he'd to do her, and when she moaned softly, his mouth absorbed it.

His hands roamed up and down her back, stopping at her butt and palming the firm globes. The woman kept in shape, and it showed. Squeezing her cheeks, he pulled her closer to him so she could feel his desire for her. At the contact, he groaned, knowing he had to get her to bed soon.

The kiss went on and on, and he felt lightheaded and drunk on the strength of it. He'd kissed plenty of women in his lifetime, but he'd never known a kiss to be so erotic and affect his dick to the point he could come just from the headiness of it.

Breaking off the kiss, he growled, "Bed." He yanked the covers down the rest of the way, tossing them to the end, not caring if they slipped off the bed. They wouldn't need them for a long time.

With a giggle, Elizabeth rushed to the other side of the bed and slid across to the middle.

He waited with one knee on the bed, curious to this fun display of hers.

She spread her arms and legs wide. "I'm yours."

Holy fucking shit. Even with his years of experience in the bedroom, she still had the ability to make him want to come well before he entered her warm, velvety center. Moisture beaded the broad head of his dick. He imagined her licking it off with her mouth. *Damn.*

Unable to resist her any longer, he crawled on the bed and leveraged himself over her. His mouth crashed down on hers, hot and urgent. After a moment, his mouth moved down her jaw to her neck, where he placed hot kisses that elicited mewling sounds from her.

After tugging gently on the lobe of her ear, he moved back down her neck and nibbled his way past her collarbone. He turned his attention to her breast and toyed and teased her nipple before he took it in his mouth, nipped lightly, and suckled.

Her back arched off the bed, and she moaned in pleasure.

A smile tugged at the corners of his mouth. Knowing what she liked, he continued teasing her breasts, giving her enough pleasure to bring out breathless pants in her.

Once she moaned again, he trailed his lips down her midsection, licking the hollow indentation of her belly button before he swept downward.

Grabbing at his shoulders, she pleaded, "No. I want you inside me. Now."

He hovered over her mound, inhaling the intoxicating scent. Already, he pictured parting her pink folds and tasting her before loving and teasing her center and the pulsating nub that would be waiting for his attention.

She gazed at him with heavy-lidded eyes. "Blake, please. I want you inside me. I've wanted it all day. Don't make me wait any longer."

Wanting to please her, he slid up and captured her mouth in a searing kiss. His cock pulsed, ready to be inside her heat. He reached down and felt the wetness between her folds. She hadn't lied about wanting him inside her, and his dick got harder than he'd ever thought it could.

"Love, you'll never wait for anything as long as I'm alive."

He settled himself between her thighs and positioned his cock at her entrance. With slow, measured movements, he rocked himself inside her tightness. Agony ripped through him at the patience it took to do this.

Elizabeth wrapped her legs around him, locking her ankles at his ass. She grabbed both cheeks, lifted herself and pushed him inside her in one swift stroke.

He snapped his head to her to check that she was okay.

A mischievous smile filled her face. "I didn't want to wait."

Neither did he, but pushing himself in like that always worried him. Sure, he'd done it before, and she'd gasped, so he'd assumed that he'd hurt her. Now that he knew better, sex with them just got a whole lot better.

Sweat beaded his forehead at the intense pleasure of being this deep inside her. He needed to move, but moving might be too much.

She writhed beneath him, and he took that as his cue. So he moved, nearly sliding out and shoving himself back in deep. He leaned down, tugging on her nipple, then held his breath when she moaned and pulled his head closer. How much torture was he to take? Hell, she hadn't even touched him yet. He knew she'd want to, and that thought had a tingle begin at the base of his spine. *Oh shit.*

Reaching down, he flipped his thumb over her clit, and she shifted and tossed her head back. He rubbed the nub and teased her nipple while managing sure strokes that kept those sexy sounds coming from her.

"Oh, Blake, I'm so close."

Thank God. His balls had already drawn tight at how erotic she felt. "Then come for me, love."

He lifted his head and kissed her, deep and hot, with all the love and desire he held for her. This woman was his world.

After a moment or two, she broke apart, her moans absorbed in their kiss.

He stroked in and out of her a few more times and went utterly still, groaning in pleasure.

It may have been ten seconds or ten minutes. Hell, he didn't know. But he came to himself atop Elizabeth and lifted his weight from her and slid to the side. Lying flat on his back, he held out an arm, and she rested her head on it and curled her body to his, her arm and leg thrown over him.

"Why didn't you tell me you wanted a quickie?" he asked with a chuckle as he stroked her soft hair. Damn, his limbs were weak.

"I didn't until you lay your naked body on mine. I held out for as long as I could." She lifted her head up and looked at him. "Is that a problem?"

A chuckle erupted from deep within his chest. "I'm a guy. There's never a problem with a quickie."

Chapter Six

Something roused Blake from a deep, sated sleep. He instinctively reached out his arm and found Elizabeth snuggled next to him. Contentment washed over him. Having her by his side made the world a better place. He loved his woman and would do anything for her.

Something niggled at him again. As he blinked his eyes a couple of times to bring his gaze into focus, he realized too late what had woken him. He stiffened as a man opened the door and peeked in. Blake could see the outline of someone behind him.

His pulse ratcheted up, and his heart pounded erratically. His thoughts went to protection—what did he have to fight them off with? He didn't have a gun or a bat or anything like that in this room. Mary and Henry were out for the night, not that they'd be a lot of help at their age. It was down to him and his fists. Thank God he hadn't let himself go soft. He might not work out as often as he did when he was younger, but he did hit the gym when his schedule permitted.

Knowing he had no defense lying prone on the bed, he slowly slid his feet from under the covers so they wouldn't get tangled up when he moved. Oh how he wished he'd slept on the other side of the bed so he'd be closer and not have the bed and Elizabeth between him and trouble.

Not caring that he was naked, he slid the covers off the rest of his body and sprang up, landing on the balls of his feet. Ready for a fight. "What do you want?" he demanded.

"Blake?" Elizabeth said sleepily from the bed. She rolled over to face him, away from the intruders. "What are you doing?"

"Love, I want you to stay still. Don't move," he said quietly but firmly. How the hell could he protect her? She was between him and the men.

There was only one option to protect her: he had to move. Slowly, he navigated to the end of the bed and was midway to Elizabeth's side and putting himself between her and the intruders when the two men, dressed in all black, walked fully into the room, switched on the light, and pulled handguns. Blake's stomach knotted in a million pieces. Was this another threat, or did they plan to kill him? Christ, had he brought this to the woman he loved? Had he put her in danger? He received so many threats it was hard to take them seriously. But one must've been serious for this to occur. Unless it was a home intrusion. He couldn't discount that idea.

Christ, he'd forgotten to set the security alarm on the house. This was his fault.

He had to talk his way out of this. "What do you want?" He held his ground but craved to move to Elizabeth.

A gasp escaped her, and he turned to see her pulling the sheet up to her neck to cover her naked body as she turned to the door. She, of course, did not stay like he'd told her. He'd known she'd do her own thing. Why had he even wasted his breath?

With as much anger as he currently held for these men holding a gun on the future Mrs. Hamilton, whether she knew it or not, didn't help him figure out how to get close enough to wrestle a gun free and pull off a ski mask so he could see who'd fucked up a perfectly good night's sleep.

"She's coming with us," the taller of the two intruders said in a deep voice with a slight southern drawl. Was he local? Blake wasn't aware of any local threats. He had an idea of the hundred or so nationwide relating to his voting record and stance on issues. Could one of them have come from here and they missed it? No, Randy was good at going through his threats and ferreting out what they really needed to worry about and getting it to the right people.

Boy, he could use his assistant—his Boy Wonder, as he referred to the kid—right about now. The boy could slip into a room completely unnoticed.

Braving it, he took another step forward. "She's not going anywhere." Another step. "Now, tell me what this is all about." Another step.

The short, pudgy man waved his weapon at Blake and narrowed his eyes. "Stop right there."

Blake froze and put his hands up in front of his chest. He wouldn't allow them to take Elizabeth. His heart pounded so hard he imagined it bursting through his ribcage. He wouldn't allow it. "If you must take someone, take me instead."

"Sorry, Senator, you have a job to do while we keep her."

"No," he said forcefully. His heart bottomed out. He had brought this to her. "Tell me what you want, and I'll do it. But don't take her."

White teeth gleamed at him through the tall intruder's smile. He stepped closer to Elizabeth and pointed his weapon at her head. "Be a good boy and do what we say, or I'll splatter her brains all over this nice bedroom."

Blake's mind went into a whirlwind. What could he do? If he complied, they'd take Elizabeth and do God only knew what. If he didn't comply, they'd kill her. Christ, this was fucked up. He wanted to rub his temples and think, but he kept his hands held steady. Something told him they wouldn't actually kill her if she was their bargaining chip, but he couldn't take the chance with her life. It'd taken him so long to find the one woman who completed him; he couldn't do anything to lose her. He could only pray they treated her well until his sons arrived and they could rescue her. Yeah, that was what he'd do. He could count on his sons to free Elizabeth. That was what they did, and they were damn good at it.

Acquiescing, he nodded. "What do you want me to do?"

"Blake?" Elizabeth's panicked voice kicked him in the gut.

He ignored her and told the man holding the gun to her head, "Let her get dressed. Privately. I promise to comply."

The tall intruder appeared to consider this. He never looked at the shorter man holding his gun on Blake. So, Tall, Dark, and Menacing was in charge. That knowledge might help Jesse. The man nodded. He stepped back from Elizabeth and waved his gun. "We'll step away for you to get dressed. Quickly. If I even perceive you are doing anything funny, I will kill him and then you."

Elizabeth gasped.

The tall man put his weapon in the back of his pants and came toward Blake. From each of his pockets, he withdrew pieces of rope. Christ. They planned to tie him up so he couldn't go after them. *Fuck. Fuck. Fuck.*

"Turn around and put your arms behind your back," he directed Blake.

With one last look at Elizabeth's fearful eyes, he complied as he'd promised. "Elizabeth, get dressed," he said while turning from her. *Please, God, don't let this be the last I ever see of her.* "I love you."

As his arms were pulled behind him and his hands tied so tight together he worried about circulation, he finally heard the bedsheets rustle, signally Elizabeth movement.

"Sit down," Tall, Dark, and Menacing demanded, pushing Blake down on the armchair in the room after he'd finished tying his hands.

While his feet were tied and with rage consuming him, Blake wanted to do nothing more than headbutt the man tying him up and find a way out of this. He wanted to inflict pain on the men who threw his and Elizabeth's lives into chaos.

Blake had already started trying to work with the knots on his wrists. No success yet, but he'd give it his full attention when the men were gone.

"Lie down on your side and pull your feet toward your ass."

Oh, fuck no. They were going to hogtie him! Fear skittered up his spine. He'd be helpless and not able to get free and start the search before his sons arrived. If no one checked on him and Elizabeth, he could be like that for days.

The intruder pulled his gun from the waistband of his pants, stepped back, and pointed it at a now-dressed Elizabeth.

"Okay, okay." Awkwardly, Blake got on the floor, trying to keep his feet far enough away to generate some slack.

The rope scratched roughly against his skin as it was looped around his feet and hands, then pulled tight, drawing his feet back into the most godawful, uncomfortable position. "What do you want from me?" Anything to get his Elizabeth back.

"Our boss will be in touch." He tightened the rope and stood.

Blake lay helpless, tied up like an animal at a rodeo. His chances of getting free flew out the window. Not that he wouldn't give up, but he was also realistic. He'd have to rely on his children to save him. That was so damn backward to how life should be for a family. All of them, except Trent, had relied on him at one point or another in their life. Maybe this was payback time. No matter what, he needed them. Not only at the house, but looking for him and Elizabeth so someone would find him. Then, they could go into warrior mode—hell, he felt it coming on himself—and they'd rescue her.

"Wait," he said, stalling, while the shorter man grabbed Elizabeth's arm. "What are you going to do with her?"

"Don't worry. You follow our boss's instructions, and she'll be returned to you unharmed. Oh, yeah, this goes without saying, but no police." The tall kidnapper switched off the lights and led the shorter man and Elizabeth out the door. Then he reached inside the door and engaged the lock.

Son of a bitch. That would keep everyone away. Knowing he couldn't let Elizabeth go without something, he shouted, "Elizabeth, do what they say and stay safe. I'll come for you."

The intruder looked as if he had an issue with his statement, and maybe he did because Blake hadn't said he'd do what they wanted. He said he'd come after her. The intruder stepped back into the room and walked over to Blake. He knelt beside him and shoved a foul-tasting cloth in Blake's mouth. With the butt of his pistol, he hit Blake on the back of the head.

Pain exploded from where the handle hit his skull and then spread out like a spiderweb, shooting agony with it. He wanted his hands to grab his head and massage it, do something to make it feel better.

"Missed." Before Blake could react, the man struck out again with the butt of his pistol. This time, he hit his mark as stars swam before Blake's eyes, and he couldn't stop the darkness from encroaching from the sides of his vision.

He closed his eyes to clear his vision and couldn't open them again as blackness took hold.

Chapter Seven

"What's up, Buttercup?" Jesse Hamilton's brother, Devon, asked their four-year-old niece, Amber, as she walked by the small couch the two men had commandeered once the fasten seatbelt sign had been turned off.

The entire family, minus Trent and Kelly, who'd travel separately from Montana, were on the large private plane bound for Oxford, Mississippi, to visit their dad for some mysterious weekend outing. Actually finding a time when everyone was available was a miracle in itself, so Jesse looked forward to whatever their dad surprised them with.

Amber's hands rushed to her hips, and she gave Devon a stern look. "Uncle Dev, you know my name is Amber, not Buttercup. Can you quit calling me all these different names and call me Amber like you're supposed to?"

Devon grinned and his shoulders shook as his fight to hold in his laughter appeared to be failing miserably. He rubbed his chin in thought. "Amber, huh?" Dropping his hand, he nodded. "Okay."

"Good," she said firmly before skipping off to her mother.

Those within earshot erupted in laughter. When the noise began to break off, Jesse asked, "Are you really going to start calling her Amber?" He hadn't since she'd been born.

"Hell, no. It's much more fun this way."

"Just don't start aggravating my daughter."

Devon shook his head. "She's too much like you and Kate. She might kick my ass for it."

At seven years old, she'd already been begging Kate to teach her how to fight. While he wanted her to be able to defend herself, Jesse hadn't figured out how he felt about it.

Jesse's twin brothers, Brad and Matt, ambled over and took the two chairs flanking the small couch. As if noticing something might happen without him, their baby brother AJ hurried away from his wife and six-month-old son.

"Why do you think Dad's doing all of this?" AJ asked, waving his arm to encompass the private airplane. They'd flown here in this level of comfort before, but that had been when they'd been transporting their sister, Emily, and her daughter, Amber, who'd been in danger. Typically when they came to Oxford, they flew commercial. It wasn't that their dad couldn't afford it. Hell, there were probably enough people who owed him favors that he got the ride for free. It was just that he did it. Jesse knew that meant he was softening them up for something.

Emily and Jake, the Hamilton foster son and Emily's husband, walked toward them. "A family meeting without us?"

Matt leaned forward, resting his arms on his thighs. "Think he's going to tell us he's retiring?"

The group remained quiet. The topic had been brought up once before, but like now, no one commented. It was as if speaking the words might make it so.

They wanted the best for their father who'd done his damnedest to raise six boys—one not even his own—and a daughter without a mother figure in the household. If they hadn't kept running off the nannies who had been hired, life would've been easier on him.

Devon braved the topic. "I don't know. But if he is, I'll support him."

Jesse almost growled. "Of course we'll all support him. It's just what brought it on."

"Do you think the secret of Trent is it?" AJ asked.

Shaking his head, Jesse sighed. "No. He plans to tell the world as soon as Trent is ready, so if it got out early, that would just piss him off, but not make him leave office."

Emily gasped. "Is there some scandal we don't know about?"

Jesse's heart pounded. That was his concern. Something his father couldn't beat. No one had said a disease because after losing their mother from cancer, they didn't want to consider something happening to their father.

Kate walked up to the group. "I know this is family time, but have you thought it might be about a woman? Hasn't he been dating the same woman for a while now?"

Awareness shot through the group, and they each sat up straight. Was their dad ready to move to the next level and marry someone? He'd been single since their mom died way too many years ago.

"I like that idea better," AJ said with a wide smile. "Let's go with it."

Before anyone could insert their opinion, the pilot

came over the speaker and told them to prepare for landing.

Jesse slipped away with Kate to ensure their two children—Jason and Reagan—were belted into their seats.

"Is this a mission?" Jason asked. They'd adopted the fourteen-year-old not long after he'd turned thirteen. While he'd been recovering from an infection due to his leukemia, the boy's parents had died. Kate had developed such a close relationship with him, Jesse couldn't do anything else but adopt him. The budding football star was an amazing kid, and Jesse was glad for every day they had with him.

Jesse pushed aside the edges of his belt buckle and sat. He turned in his seat while he picked up the belt. "What makes you say that?"

A half-hearted shrug lit Jason's shoulders. "I saw you all meeting."

With a shake of his head, Jesse turned back around. "No. We were just making plans." And they were, each silent with how they'd deal with whatever this trip tossed at them. At least this time they hadn't had to bring their equipment.

After they'd landed and taxied the small airport at Oxford, he stepped onto the stairs and looked around. It was a habit he never expected to lose. In his sweep of the area, he saw the four minivans waiting for them. What he didn't see was their father. He stepped down the stairs expecting that he was just running late. They still had to unload and get all of those damn car seats and booster seats set up.

By the time the family was loaded up, Jesse had called their father's phone six times and received no answer. Even texts went unanswered.

A rock hit the pit of his stomach. This wasn't like his father. Either Blake Hamilton had a big-ass surprise waiting for them or something wasn't right. He swallowed past the lump forming in his throat. Something told him it was the latter.

****

As the minivans pulled into the long drive of the Hamilton Oxford home, Jesse noticed that it did so behind a blue sedan that stopped in front of the house. He smiled when Trent stepped from the obvious rental and waved before he opened the back door. Little Ashley would be with him and Kelly. Seeing Trent as a father about floored him as much as it did when AJ became one. Big men fall hard for little ones. Hell, he'd probably been just as mushy when Reagan had been a baby.

Having Trent here would mean a lot to their father. Although Trent wouldn't admit it, Jesse felt it meant a lot to Trent also. With the man who raised him dead, a gaping hole remained in Trent's life. Blake could fill that better than anyone else. If Trent allowed it.

When the lead van, carrying Jesse and his family, came to a halt, he opened the door and jumped out, needing to see his father for some reason. That tight grip around his gut wouldn't ease. He glanced at the open front door and only saw Mary, the housekeeper they all loved as part of the family. No Blake Hamilton.

Christ, could the surprise really be his health and he was stuck in bed, unable to greet them? Could he be dying? A fist clenched over his heart at the thought of losing their father. Oh, it'd happen one day, but Jesse preferred it to be when Blake was old and ready to move on.

Trying to remain calm for his family, he turned around and began helping them out of the van. His eyes almost misted at Reagan in her booster seat. In one more year, she'd be out of it. Depending on the state they were driving in at the time. Either way, she'd grown up so damn fast. Hell, she was already in the second grade. He wanted it to stop. Wanted her to stay young and innocent.

"Daddy, I can't get out with you in the way."

Jesse started. He hadn't realized he'd been blocking her exit while dreaming about her remaining young. She'd undone her own seat belt—something she'd learned way too early—and was ready to jump down. Instead, he grabbed her under her arms and swung her around to stand behind him. Her giggle about undid him. It was the sweetest sound he'd ever heard.

"I think I can get out on my own," Kate said, poking her head out.

Oh hell no. Not after that statement. He reached up, grasped her under her arms, pulled her out of the van, and swung her around. Her laughter was the second sweetest sound to his ears.

"Um, I really can get down by myself."

Jesse released Kate and spun around to Jason. He grinned, and when it made his son a bit nervous, he stepped back out of the way. "By all means."

A loud sigh of relief hissed from inside the van before Jason disembarked.

After seeing their luggage being unloaded, the family swarmed the entrance to the house and one waiting woman.

"Hello, Mary." Jesse pulled her up into a bear hug, her feet dangling in the air.

When he set her down, AJ picked the woman up and swung her around, narrowly missing the family members. AJ placed her back on her feet and planted a big kiss on her cheek. "Hello, Mary."

When Mary and Henry had started working for their dad, AJ had still been young and impressionable. With her being the closest thing to a mother figure he'd had, the two had bonded closer than any of the other members of the family, even with Emily, who was the youngest.

More hugs were administered and introductions were made. Yet, no Dad. He didn't like this at all.

Once most of the family had dispersed, Jesse asked Mary, "Where's Dad?" It wasn't like him to not only miss seeing them at the airport like he'd said he'd do but to not greet them at the door. Something had to be wrong.

A blush exploded on the older woman's face. Wasn't there an age when blushing stopped? Well, apparently not if Mary was capable of it.

"He's with his lady."

By Jesse's side, Kate did a fist pump. "Yes! I got it right."

He held back his chuckle at her exuberance. A woman. Someone who was so important he didn't greet the family he'd invited. One slice of relief hit him when he realized that meant no terminal disease. "Have they not been down this morning?" he directed at Mary.

As she fidgeted with the white apron she wore, Mary shook her head. "No."

Furrowing his brows in concentration, Jesse took a

deep breath to still his racing heart. No. No matter how much into this woman his dad was, he wouldn't forget his children. If, by chance, that was the truth, then they wouldn't want her to be part of their father's life. "Did you knock on their door?"

Another blush. Hell. "I did when I saw the first car turn in the drive. All I heard was…a moan." Her voice changed to a whisper. "I didn't want to interrupt their…well, you know."

A moan and nothing else. His pulse rate rocketed and his palms grew sweaty. He took off at a run to the staircase and his father's room. Something was definitely wrong.

He pounded on the door with his fist.

His brothers arrived in a rush behind him.

"What's going on, Jesse?" Matt asked.

"Shh," he directed. Only a low moan. He checked the doorknob. Locked. No problem, he had enough adrenaline rushing through his veins right now to lift the house if necessary. Stepping back, he charged at the door with his shoulder. Wood splintered around the frame, but it didn't give. Dammit for solid woodsmanship.

He stepped back to do it again and Matt stopped him. "Let me."

No need to argue because Matt doing it made more sense. Brad and Matt busted the shit out of players on the scrimmage line when they had played football in high school and college. As a former SEAL, Matt kept in shape, so this would be child's play for him.

Sure enough, Matt broke the door on his first try. Mind, Jesse had helped loosen it.

They rushed into the room to find their father,

naked and tied up. That was just what he wanted to see—his father naked. No one wanted to see their parents in the buff. Then again, he also preferred not to see his father tied up like a pig ready to roast.

Jesse pulled the cloth from his father's mouth while someone behind him opened a knife. With the cloth free, their father rubbed his tongue in his mouth a few times before speaking with a rough, raspy tone. "They have Elizabeth."

Who the fuck is Elizabeth? And who the fuck is they? he almost said out loud. He had to wait to ask those questions until their dad was free.

"Let's get you untied, Dad," Jesse said while Brad cut through the ropes.

It seemed to take forever for Brad to cut through everything. Jason, who'd snuck in, rubbed his grandfather's ankles once they were loose while their dad rubbed his wrists that were raw from where he'd obviously tried to get free.

AJ dropped a pair of jeans, underwear, and a blue shirt onto their father's lap, thankfully covering his junk. It was hard to think of his dad being in here and with a woman. Not that he couldn't do something like that, but thinking about it was pure gross.

Knowing his legs would be weak from being in that position for so long, Jesse helped his father stand and stood beside him while he dressed. Just in case he needed the help. Jesse also checked his father's body over—discreetly—for any wounds he might've endured.

Nothing. Just tied up and—

Blake rubbed his neck, and Jesse peered closer. Big-ass goose egg. The intruders must've knocked him out also. Jesus Christ, tying him up as they had and stuffing a rag in his mouth hadn't been enough? Did they expect him to turn into Superman and break through his bonds with his super strength?

His pissed-off factor just notched up a couple of rungs of an invisible ladder. It was close to teetering over the edge. Yet he needed a calm and level head to deal with whatever had happened here.

Matt reentered the room with a glass of water and handed it to their father.

"Here," Matt said before stepping back. "This will help your parched mouth and throat. That rag couldn't have been comfortable."

Of course Matt would think of that. The training he'd undergone as a SEAL meant learning to endure all kinds of torturous shit. A rag in the mouth probably didn't even register to him.

"Thank you, son," Blake rasped before he downed the glass in one large gulp.

Once he finished, he dropped down on the bed and ran a hand over his face. "I need your help."

That much was fucking obvious, but Jesse kept that fact to himself. "Go ahead, Dad. We're here for you."

"Someone broke in here last night and kidnapped the woman I love. The woman I wanted you to meet this weekend." His voice broke as he spoke. "I need you to get her back. She's everything to me. I can't lose her."

Well, son of a bitch. Their vacation has just turned into a HIS mission.

Chapter Eight

Blake had never been happier to see his children as he was at that moment. Not only to rescue him but because he knew they could save Elizabeth. He didn't trust the kidnappers to keep their word on not hurting her. Plus, he had no idea when this mysterious boss planned to tell him what he wanted.

The whole idea of her being someone's captive sickened him. His brain flew through all the terrible things that could happen at the hands of those two men. He could only pray none of them touched her. That, and get her the hell away from them as soon as possible.

Feeling self-conscious with everyone crowding him in his bedroom, he decided it was time to move to where they'd all fit. Comfortably. "Let's go to the family room. If you could keep the children away, that'd be best."

Most of them nodded as they filed out of the room. He stayed behind for a second, looking at the bed. The bed he and Elizabeth had made love in before—

He swore. His heart had been ripped out when they'd taken her away from him. He'd do whatever it took to get her back. Whatever it took.

With that decided, he strode out of his room to seek the help he needed.

In the noisy living room, Blake was surprised to see not only his sons but also Emily and their spouses.

And Trent. Joy flooded his system. He hadn't been sure if Trent would actually come, but he did, and having his entire family there to support him made him weak in the knees. There were so many family members now that they'd run out of space for everyone to sit, so a couple of his sons had their wives on their laps, and his single sons—Matt and Brad—stood awkwardly beside them. Their time would come, he was certain. They'd find the right women. Sadness tried to seep in for Matt because he'd once found the woman he wanted to spend his life with, but....

It was then his family noticed him, and everything quieted down. He swallowed past the lump forming in his throat. Where to start? Something easy would work. "Where are the children?" Surely they didn't just drop them somewhere for Jason to watch over. There was an infant in the mix. One he'd yet to see and wanted to rush to wherever his new granddaughter was, but this came first, so he held fast.

"Mary offered to watch them," Kate said from beside Jesse, their hands entwined.

"Ashley?" he asked with a croak in his voice.

"She's okay. Kelly just fed her so we're good for a little while," Trent said with Kelly in his lap.

Blake nodded for lack of what else to do.

"Dad," Jesse said, "what happened?"

His gaze scanned the room. "I can't call the police, or they'll hurt her. I don't know how serious they are, but I won't take the chance. I need your help. I need HIS." Never in his wildest dreams had he ever thought he'd have to ask his sons for help. Especially not this kind of help. Being proud of the men your sons had become was one thing. Asking them to do whatever is necessary to rescue the love of your life was another. But there was no other option until he found out what the kidnapper wanted.

"You've got it," Jesse said it, but his other sons and Emily nodded along with the statement. Sometimes he forgot she'd become part of the group. Her not wielding a weapon allowed her to slip from his mind. Stupid of him since, from what he'd learned, she was a strong partner. Pride enveloped him at her showing her big brothers how worthy she was. That unwavering support almost brought tears to his eyes.

"Last night, two men broke into the house and kidnapped Elizabeth and tied me up."

"What about Mary and Henry?" AJ asked, worry crowding his voice.

Shaking his head, he blew out a sigh. "I sent them out for the night. They stayed with their daughter." Relief at their being safe washed through him. Who knew what the kidnappers would've done to them? "I forgot to set the alarm before we went to bed."

Ignoring his lapse in judgment, Jesse asked, "What else happened?" Blake had known his eldest son would take the lead on questioning. He's always looked after his siblings. It didn't go unnoticed by Blake, but he wished Jesse hadn't had to do it because he worked so much. If only Blake could go back in time. Then he'd what? Resign? That was what would've been required to spend the time he wanted with his children.

When he hadn't been working, he'd spent as much time as he could with them. That meant missing out on important parties and such. But his children came first when he wasn't required to be in Congress.

He put his hands in his pockets and swayed a bit,

not wishing to appear weak. Without a weapon or his sons' defensive training, he couldn't think of anything he could've done better.

"Elizabeth and I were asleep. I woke to a noise and saw two men—dressed in all black, head to toe—entering the bedroom. I jumped out of bed to confront them, but I had no weapon and they had handguns." He swallowed against the loss lodged painfully in his throat. "They tied me up and took Elizabeth."

"Was she okay when they took her?" Kate asked.

He nodded. "Yeah. Thank God they allowed her to dress first."

Knowing smiles passed between a couple of the women. What was that for? Had they known he planned to introduce them to their new stepmother or stepmother-in-law?

"What did they want?" Jesse asked sternly.

A rush of breath escaped him as his shoulders sagged. "That's just it. They told me to wait for their boss's order."

Jesse's jaw worked before he spoke. "Maybe we'll get something today. In the meantime, we'll check things out here and see if we can get a clue that will help. We'll also need more information from you on what you're working on and who this Elizabeth is."

"She's about to be your stepmother," he spat out. Hell, he hadn't meant to tell them that way. He'd wanted them to get to know her and love her like he did. "I mean, once I ask her, that is."

There were smiles, but he imagined they were a bit hesitant because of the situation. Emily was the first to jump up and hug him. "I'm so happy for you, Dad. The team will bring her home."

When he released her, all of his sons stood. Each took their turn to congratulate him and promise to return her as soon as possible. Their support choked him up, and they hadn't even met her. They were truly happy—for him. No jealousy from the marriage with their mother or anything of the sort. They truly supported him. The knowledge infused him with a pride and love he'd never thought could get greater. But it had. Now they needed to complete his family.

Megan—AJ's wife—and Kelly discreetly left the room. Whether it was because they weren't part of the team or for the children, it didn't matter. Even though they were both reporters, he didn't worry they'd splash this in the media. They'd always kept quiet about family business.

Jesse barked orders and he listened to the workings of the team. Even though Trent was no longer part of HIS, he stayed and offered his help. A lightness pulsed in his heart at that show of unity.

"Brad and Matt, see what you can find from their path."

"We don't have anything to check for prints," Matt replied.

"We'll do what we can. I don't think we have anything yet."

"I have my weapon. It was in my suitcase." Kate offered.

"Me, too," AJ added.

"Me, too," came from every other member of the team. Devon, Brad, Matt, Jake, and Rylee—their newest member.

Jesse shook his head after every team member present piped in, and by the look on his face, he'd done the same thing too.

What the hell had they expected on this trip? For that matter, did they do this on any non-HIS trips they took where they could manage to sneak in their weapon? Like on a private charter. Hell, he couldn't say anything about how inappropriate it was since he wanted them to have their weapons on this trip.

He was also secretly glad Emily hadn't joined the fray. He didn't think he could handle her in danger like that. Kate and Rylee had trained for it. They knew what to expect. His baby girl was just that in his mind.

"Dad." Jesse's voice pulled him from his musings. "We need a plane on standby in case we find out they took her somewhere else."

Thank God there was something he could do. Yet it wasn't enough. "I'll take care of it." He waited a minute, then added, "Whatever happens, I want to be in on it. I want to be there when you rescue her."

Quiet blanketed the room, enough to almost stifle his breathing. The occupants kept looking at each other as if in silent communication. Maybe they were, and that was part of why they were so successful in what they did.

"Dad—" Jesse started.

"Don't give me any of that Dad crap. I can help, and I promise not to get in the way." His gaze swept the room, his stare intent. "Remember when those of you who are married had your wives in harm's way? Would you have allowed yourself to be sidelined and let someone else protect her?"

Jesse hissed out a long breath. "Okay."

Yes. Success.

"But only if you listen to everything we say and

not get in the way," Jesse finished.

"Jesse, I know we have our handguns, but I'd feel much better with my arsenal if we're doing a rescue," Brad said.

Another round of "Me, too" sounded.

Turning to him, Jesse said, "Can you get someone to fly our equipment—no questions asked—from Baltimore to here? Like yesterday? I can have Ken have it ready for shipment as soon as you can get a plane ready."

Although he didn't want to wait that long to go after Elizabeth, he saw their need for the equipment since this had started at gunpoint. "Consider it done," Blake said.

The men coordinated longer, and Blake became more impressed with them. There wasn't much they could do at this point, but that didn't stop the team. He answered questions on what he was doing at Congress, filling them in on all the threats he'd recently received.

His phone rang, and the room quieted as everyone froze, their eyes on him. With shaking hands, he removed his phone from his pocket and looked at the screen. "It's just my assistant," he told them. With a sense of relief, yet impatience at Elizabeth's captors not calling, he answered the phone. "Hey, Randy. I'm a little busy. Can this wait?"

"I don't think so. There's an e-mail that I think you need to know about," Randy said. "It's about Elizabeth."

Chapter Nine

As her kidnappers helped her exit the car, Elizabeth tried to make out more than shapes through the black cloth bag one of the men had tossed over her head before they'd left Blake's house, each holding one of her arms in a tight grasp so she couldn't escape. She'd witnessed them removing their masks, but with the density of the material and the fact it was still dark outside, she couldn't make out their features. Not even the color of their hair.

A part of her rejoiced that they prevented her from seeing them. Wasn't it that if they allowed you to see them, they planned to kill you? At least it was that way on the silver screen. Still, bile rose in her throat wondering if she would survive. If this would be her end because some maniac wanted Blake to do something.

Without a doubt, she knew Blake would do everything in his power to rescue her or do whatever it was they wanted. Her heart sank that he might have to compromise his values to save her.

Her thoughts went to how the men had left him. He'd been tied up and left inside the room. When would he be found? Would he be okay? Concern for him swamped her and pulled away some of her fear over her predicament.

Yeah, she feared what might happen. She'd be

stupid not to do so. But she'd tried to be smart by listening and even struggling to make out the outline of the landscape, anything that could help her escape. Because, unless they held a gun directly on her the entire time, she would try to escape.

Now she wished she'd paid more attention to heroines in movies and what they actually did to save themselves. Even some of the fight moves would be welcome. Although she doubted she could overpower these two.

"Step up," one of her kidnappers said a bit too late.

Walking blindly sucked, she thought as she hit her toes on the edge of a step—concrete by the hardness of it and the sharp pain shooting up her foot. They let her dress, but they hadn't given her time to put on shoes.

"I said step up," the man growled as she reached down and held her toes in her hand, rubbing to soothe away the throbbing pain. At least she hadn't broken any of them. She wondered what they'd have done if she had. Would they take her to a hospital or make her suffer in silence? Her money was on the latter.

"This would be a lot easier if I could see," she demanded with all the power she could force into her words.

"Shut up and step up. You've got three of them."

They managed to navigate the stairs without further incident, except the bruises she was sure to have from where they'd gripped her arms to make sure she stepped up at the right moment. She really hated these bastards.

A door opened in front of her and she was ushered into the house. She assumed it was a house based on what she could glean.

"I'm picking you up and carrying you," a deep voice said. "If you try to harm me, I'll drop your ass and shoot you."

Several inappropriate comments tried to spew from her mouth, but she reined them in as he pulled her into his arms and bounded up a flight of stairs. Now it made sense why he carried her after their fiasco with three lousy stairs outside.

He didn't drop her at the top of the stairs. When he set her down, she stood in front of a door that her captor reached around and opened. "Get in."

Panic seized her in its tight grasp, cutting off her air supply. What kind of prison was this? A hand on her back pushed her forward, and she lost her footing, just catching it before she face-planted. The door slammed behind her and she heard a distinct click of a lock. They'd locked her in from the outside.

Reaching up, she ripped the bag from her head and blinked with watery eyes until her gaze became accustomed to the light. Slowly spinning around, she surveyed her surroundings. A lump climbed into her throat and almost choked her. This room was set up for a woman, with pink as the primary color. The double bed had a lovely rose-covered quilt, and a vase of roses sat at the bedside. On the dresser across the room, figurines of ballerinas held a prominent place.

Her gaze settled on the window and she rushed to it. They'd driven for a long time, so she'd never make the walk back on foot, but she still had to try to get free. Excitement washed over her and her heart pounded. Freedom.

After searching for any alarms and finding none, she reached down to pull the window up. Two things hit her at once. She was on the second floor so she'd have to jump from the window and the nails holding it closed would've prevented even that desperate feat.

Her heart sank like a lead ball to her stomach, rolling around until she was queasy. She was truly trapped in here for God knew how long. With a gut-wrenching sob, she dropped onto the bed, buried her face in her hands and cried.

It was still hard to believe this was happening. She'd been in bed with Blake—the man she loved more than life. If her friend Crystal had been right and he'd planned to propose, this sidelined that idea for her rescue.

She sniffed and smiled, thinking of Blake and the last time they'd snuck away to his home for an evening together. She'd walked in, completely surprised and pleased, to see him wearing a cooking apron and holding tongs.

"There are times when I want to cook my meal, and this is one of them."

"Why?" she'd asked. "What makes it different today?"

With a seductive smile, he'd closed in on her and dropped a kiss on her lips before she could protest. "Because I get to cook for you." He'd winked and turned to the back door where she'd seen the grill.

He'd cooked for her. Blake had always treated her like a princess, but that act had felt different in their relationship.

Their relationship. Did he plan to bring them out in the open? Everything he'd said and done made her feel like they were moving to a new level.

Of course, this inconvenience wasn't going to help.

Yes, she called it an inconvenience because Blake would find a way to rescue her. He'd talked about the organization his children owned. Without meeting her, she knew that they'd help because it was their father, and if they loved him even half as much as he loved them, they'd do anything for him.

Blake, I won't give up finding a chance to escape, but my money is on you rescuing me.

Chapter Ten

Blake's hands shook like a leaf, and his heart pounded in fear. "Read it to me."

Picking up on his distress, Jesse mouthed, "Put it on speaker."

After doing that, he held it out enough so Randy could hear him, but the group could also hear Randy. A goddamn e-mail. Her captor had to be an idiot. His son Devon could trace that in a heartbeat. Sure, some of the threats he'd received had been untraceable, but Devon hadn't been on them. He had full faith in his son's abilities.

"It says, 'Get the rephase of the A10 passed, and Elizabeth goes free.' What's going on, Senator? Is she in trouble? Has something happened to Elizabeth?"

Randy was the one person who knew about his relationship with Elizabeth. Not only did he trust the kid, his assistant needed to know what Blake was doing when he was off the grid.

"What's that mean, Dad?" Jesse asked. "I thought they were phasing out the A10s since they were so old and parts were too expensive."

He nodded. That was the current plan, but the timeline for the replacement fighter had slipped. That tidbit hadn't been made public yet. Yet someone had gotten hold of it and was pushing for the extension. Even if they didn't agree to one, they'd be fine. Not as strong as they could be, but the A10s, while badass aircraft, had antiquated systems that did the pilots a disservice when in the air. As a member of the Senate Appropriations Committee, and Chairman of the Defense Subcommittee, he had intimate knowledge of the project and wanted to give it good consideration. But now this.

He pulled the phone to his ear. "Don't worry, Randy. Everything will be fine."

Amidst a choked protest, he disconnected the call and replaced the phone in his pants pocket.

To Jesse, he said, "It is. However, it's only recently been brought to the committee to extend that timeline. I can't figure out if the military or the parts manufacturers are the biggest proponents of the idea. It's still new, but it's getting a great deal of attention since there're advocates for both sides of the situation."

"Where do you stand on it?" Matt asked with a hint of true curiosity in his voice.

Blake shrugged, and a slice of anger threaded through him at why she'd been taken. For political or financial reasons. Why couldn't they just hold her for ransom? He'd empty his bank accounts and investments to see her safe. Instead, they want him to compromise himself. Possibly because they have no idea where he stood. But he wasn't the person to approve or deny. He was just one vote. To get her back, he'd have to convince others without sharing why. His stomach soured at that idea. He'd always led with his conscience.

"I haven't seen all of the information, but I'm not opposed to it so far." That much was true. "Only as long as we can provide safe aircraft for the men and women who fly them."

"How are the others on the issue?" Jesse queried. "The vote?" he added.

He shook his head in bewilderment. "I don't know how the other committee members stand. We haven't really discussed it yet. As for the vote, it's not for two weeks." He stared at his eldest son. "God, I can't leave her with them for two weeks." Two weeks of no telling what she was enduring hit him full force in the chest, almost knocking him to the ground. Would they respect her and treat her like a guest? Or would they abuse her and treat her like an unwelcome prisoner? He mentally sent up a silent prayer for the first one.

"Why kidnap her so early?" Emily asked.

"My guess is so he can use the time to sway the other committee members to his way of thinking. Or to the kidnappers' way of thinking," Jesse offered.

"I'm in."

Blake hadn't even noticed Devon had been on his computer the entire time. "In what?"

A grin split his son's face. "Your e-mail."

He didn't know whether to be proud or pissed at the intrusion. He knew his son could do anything; he'd just rather not hear of the illegal things he did—like hack into a senator's government e-mail account. "Don't get into trouble, son. My clout only goes so far."

Staring down at the keys rapidly typing on a keyboard, Devon replied, "Don't worry about it. They won't even know I was there."

"What do you want us to do, Dad?" Jesse asked.

"Get her back as soon as possible."

"We'll do everything we can to bring her home to you."

He noticed his son left off bringing her home alive. He buried his head in his hands. *Stay safe, Elizabeth. We'll come for you.* He looked up, a firm resolve settling in him. "When you go, I'm going with you," he reiterated his statement from earlier. They would not be allowed to forget he'd be participating. He knew they tried to protect him, and while he'd been black ops when he was much younger and his skills might be rusty, some things you never forgot.

Before anyone could attempt to argue, Devon cursed. "The e-mail has been rerouted several times. I can't stay in long enough to track this without exposing myself. If I can even find it." He looked around the group. "Whoever did this is good."

That hit Blake like a sucker punch to the gut. If they couldn't track the e-mail, how would they find her? It wasn't like they left tracks after departing the house. Elizabeth hadn't had a bag of beans or something to leave a trail. They had nothing.

A hand settled on his shoulder, and he turned to see Jesse. "Don't worry, Dad. We'll find her." The hand squeezed and Blake nodded. He wouldn't give up.

"Okay. What do we do?" He looked at his watch. She has been in the bastards' hands for more than twelve hours. His stomach was sickened thinking how she might be faring.

"Let's see if we can figure out who has the biggest stake in this. I think that if we keep the aircraft in the fleet for longer than planned, people have to order parts. We'll start with the major suppliers and see what we get. They can't be too happy the government is cutting their income in a few years. Extending it would be beneficial to them."

"What can I do?" Blake asked.

"You know the political players. Think the names over. Who might be pushing this? Who might benefit from it? Anything that is a red flag."

With a nod, he turned to walk away but halted for a moment. "One of you can come with me, and I'll get you paper and such."

"Dad, we need that jet in Baltimore ready ASAP," Jesse informed him.

He'd almost forgotten his promise. Dammit, he needed Elizabeth home. With him. So they could be a family. "I'll do it as soon as I distribute the office supplies."

Emily followed him, and after entering his office, he loaded her up with notepads, pens, and pencils. "We're going to print in here, so I'll be quiet when I slip back in for the printouts." She smiled weakly at him. "They'll get her, Dad. You don't need to go."

His baby girl was protecting him. How strange his world had gotten. Never in a million years would he have imagined such a thing. His sweet, little girl—well, not so little now—trying to take care of him. His heart expanded with love. "I'm going. I have to. Jake wouldn't stay back when you were in danger. I can't just sit back. It'll kill me to wait. It's killing me now, but that...that waiting would be my undoing." He kissed her on the top of her blonde head, so like her mother's. "Don't worry, I trust my sons to have my six."

When she left, he could've sworn her eyes glistened with unshed tears. He knew they'd rather he sat back and let them handle it. And he would. To an extent.

He put his mind to the tasks he'd been assigned. After an hour, he'd come up with nothing. No one was going out of their way to make the rephase happen. And he'd have a hard battle if he had to fight for it. He hadn't been lying when he'd said he had no idea how the other committee members would vote. There'd been comments here and there—keeping the fleet to a certain size until replacements were in place and getting rid of something so out-of-date that it puts pilots at risk. Neither side was wrong, but the A10 was still quite useful.

Realizing he'd get nowhere, he strode out of his office to see how his sons had progressed. Part curiosity led his trek. He had no idea the extent of what they could do and was interested to see, to be prouder than he already was, if that were possible.

Entering the family room, which looked more like a planning room since card tables had been erected and were covered in printouts. Side tables had also been brought out, and Emily had joined Devon with her own laptop. His eyes misted.

Waiting until he was noticed, he informed them that he had nothing that would help.

"We have a starting point," Jesse told him. "There are three major manufacturers for the A10. It appears they each fought when the decision was made to retire it."

Scooting closer, Blake glanced over the sheets he hadn't even realized Emily had slipped in and collected from his printer. "Does one company have more stake in it than another?"

"No." Jesse turned to him. "We'll just have to check them all. It might take a bit longer, but we'll do it, Dad."

He nodded his belief in their ability to do this.

"We believe it'd be an owner versus the CEO, which is the same person in one case, but we won't completely discount it. We're just starting there. Have you ever had any problems with any of these owners?"

Jesse handed him a list, but it was like reading Greek. He couldn't stop his adrenaline from racing through his system at the possibility of them finding Elizabeth. After finally focusing his eyeballs on the names, he sighed in defeat. He knew some of them, but couldn't fathom them in this situation. He handed the sheet back to Jesse but grabbed it back from his grasp. "Wait a minute. If I'm not mistaken, Regina Franklin, who owns Franklin Aerodynamics, is the mother of Larry Thornton, who owns Thornton Enterprises. If my memory is correct, she's in a nursing home and requires constant care, and he oversees everything for her."

"If that's the case, Larry Thornton pretty much owns two-thirds of the market. I'd imagine he'd be pretty pissed if it all went away." Jesse shuffled the papers, looking closely at the two companies.

"He's bid for the new fighter, but I haven't heard what happened," Blake offered

"Either he didn't get it and is drawing this out until he finds something else, or he's one greedy son of a bitch," Devon bit out.

"Well, no matter his reason, he just became our number one person of interest." Jesse turned to Devon. "Dev, see what you can get. I want to know his properties and anything else that will help. Make sure to dig deep."

Devon nodded and retreated to his laptop.

"Dad, we need everything you know about Larry Thornton," Jesse demanded.

"I don't know. I've only met him once. And I didn't really like him when I did." The knowledge of his screw-up sucker-punched him in the gut. "He might've been near when I invited Elizabeth to come here with me." He groaned at his stupidity. "I broke my own rule to keep personal business away from a public affair."

Chapter Eleven

Despair tried to seep into her bones, making her body and heart heavy. With everything she had, she fought it. Elizabeth may not have found a way out, but she wouldn't give up hope. Her body was tired, but she refused to go to sleep. It didn't matter that she'd only had a couple of hours before she'd been kidnapped, she would not allow herself to be at their mercy without realizing what was happening.

Startled out of her thoughts, it took her a moment to realize there was a knock on the door. A knock. How unexpected. Then a voice boomed, "Go into the bathroom, and if you try anything, I'll shoot you. Nothing says I have to keep you alive."

Fear skittered up her spine, and her breath caught. Not wishing to risk what the man said, she scooted to the en suite on the far side of the room.

The door opened and a man wearing a ski mask entered. Again a small relief at their hiding their identities swept through her. Oh, she'd love to nail the bastards who did this, but if they hid, her chance of release was higher.

That was what she kept reminding herself.

With a tray in hand, he moved to the dresser to set it down.

Her eyes darted to the open door and hope blossomed. Could she make it? It'd be a narrow path past him. She could try. Then she noticed the weapon on his belt. No, he said he'd shoot her. It wasn't a risk she could take.

"Eat up," he said and then left.

She'd missed breakfast and had a feeling this was a late lunch. With no watch or clock and not being skilled enough to read the sun, she had no idea what time it was. But she was hungry. She took a step toward the meal and then stopped. What if they tried to drug her? Didn't some kidnappers do that?

Her mind whirled with how long she could go without food and water. Blake had to rescue her soon.

Not wanting to consider what could happen to her, she focused on what she needed to do when Blake saved her.

They were getting married. There was no doubt in her mind about that. If there was doubt in his, she'd find a way to dispose of that doubt.

Moving to the bed, she perched on its edge, her attention split between the door and the window.

A nice, small wedding—well, as small as one can get with the size of his family. *Family.* She wished with all her heart that her daughter, Melinda, was alive to witness it. Melinda had died so young from Diamond Blackfan Anemia. It was why she'd taken up the cause.

So few people understood the disease or knew what to watch for in their children's health. They'd found it early in Melinda, but with years of treatment— at the hospital and at home—she still passed away at ten years old.

A tear glided down her cheek at the loss of someone so precious to her. When someone recommended that she check into the Make-A-Wish

Foundation, she'd almost broken down. And she'd always remained strong for herself and her daughter. That type of suggestion only meant one thing—her time was getting near. That had been something she hadn't been prepared to handle. But she'd managed it outside of her closed bedroom door.

Melinda had surprised her with her choice of a Disney cruise. When she'd questioned her daughter, she'd said she wanted to see Minnie Mouse, and she knew that her mother had wanted a cruise. That time, she'd broken down and cried while she'd held her daughter.

The daughter knew her fate yet remained strong, not allowing the woes of the world to stop her.

Less than a year after the cruise, Melinda had gone to see the angels she swore were waiting for her.

With the back of her hand, Elizabeth swiped at the tears that streamed down her cheeks. She missed her little girl.

Melinda would've loved Blake. Her husband had died while their daughter was still young, so she'd never really had a father figure. Not in the years when it would've made an impact on her memories.

A knock sounded, and she automatically scuttled off the bed and huddled in the bathroom. The same command came, and she waited. Again, a man in a mask entered. He removed the tray, not commenting on her not eating, and turned to leave.

"What do you want with me?" she bravely asked, even though her limbs shook like a leaf.

"I don't know. I'm just the hired help." He continued on his way.

When he reached the door, she forced out, "How

long are you keeping me?"

The man stopped and turned. "As long as it takes," he ground out and exited, slamming the door behind him.

Returning to her perch on the bed, she waited while her heart rate settled and her body stopped trembling. Maybe she should try to rush him when he first enters. His hands would be full. She could grab the gun.

What then? She had no idea where she was or had any way to get back to Blake.

She'd said she wouldn't stop trying to find a way to escape, and she hadn't. She just sucked at it.

"It hasn't even been a full day, and I've had enough of this. Blake, get your ass here. I'm tired of waiting."

In her mind, she knew how unrealistic his coming this quick would be. They'd left him tied up. Someone would have to find him. His kids would, but how long would they wait once they'd arrived? Then he'd have to find out where she was. There was the stickler in her plans. How would they possibly find her?

Maybe he'd have to do what they wanted. She didn't know how she felt about that. Sure, she wanted to be released, but she didn't want him to not be true to himself. Not for her sake.

With nothing else to do, her mind wrapped itself around those thoughts like a yo-yo going back and forth on how she felt. The result was that she'd rather stay captive than Blake change a vote for her. She'd just wait until he figured out where she was.

She loved him too much to ask for anything different.

Noticing the sky getting darker, she stared at the

shower in the en suite and wished she could brave it. No way would she get naked for these bastards. They hadn't touched her, but who was to say it wouldn't happen?

When the knock sounded for what she expected to be dinner, she hurried to the bathroom, not wishing to cause any problems since things had been smooth so far. The voice surprised her this time.

"There's a brush and such in the bathroom. Tidy yourself up. You're having dinner in the dining room."

Fear froze her in place, sliding icicles through her veins. Eat outside her little prison? Where she'd see people and things she shouldn't. *Oh no. This was bad. Very, very bad. Anytime now, Blake would be nice.*

"You've got five minutes to get ready."

Get ready? For what? Her death sentence? She'd like a hell of a lot more time to prepare for that. She exhaled a long sigh. She could do this. Maybe she was overreacting.

Looking at the counter, she looked at the items she'd spied earlier in her inspection—brush, toothbrush, toothpaste, lotion, and perfume. Did they really think she'd want to wear perfume for someone who'd snatched her from her bed—naked—then dragged her to God knows where and treated her like a prisoner? These people had lost their blasted minds.

At the sound of the knock, she set down the brush. She'd taken advantage of all but the perfume, and she did feel better—more human.

The man entered wearing a ski mask.

Her breath whooshed from her in relief. Maybe it wouldn't be so bad. She'd at least get to make out her surroundings in the house in case they ever did something stupid like leave her door unlocked.

Led down the hall by a tall man she thought might have been one of her kidnappers, she kept her face forward, but her gaze swept the room, left to right and back again. She didn't want to miss a thing.

So focused on taking in the hallway and the number of doors, she almost missed the first step. That was all she needed, to tumble down a flight of stairs while in captivity.

As they made their descent, her pulse accelerated, and her heart pounded in worry and dread. She tried to tell herself she was stupid for those emotions, but she couldn't help it. Nothing about this situation was right.

"This way," her guard directed as he turned right after the last step.

Still scanning the room, she caught the Southern charm in the furniture and decor. What would a true Southerner need from Blake? He was a senator for Maryland.

With that thought turning over in her mind, she almost missed her guard stopping. "In there." He put his hand on the small of her back and shoved her through an opening into a formal dining room.

Wanting to turn back and kick his ass for manhandling her, she started to do just that until she realized someone else was in the room—without something covering his face.

Panic flooded her system, turning her limbs to jelly. Was this her captor? It had to be. Her stomach churned like a high sea. He was letting her see him. That meant he wasn't letting her go.

"Hello, Ms. Page. May I call you Elizabeth?" He continued without waiting for her response, "I'm Larry Thornton. Welcome to my home."

Chapter Twelve

"Give me one of those," Blake directed to Devon.

With a flashbang grenade that had arrived on the plane from Baltimore with the HIS gear in his hand, Devon looked at him in question. "Um."

"Dad, do you even know how to use one of those?" Jesse asked.

Damn his sons. He wanted all the firepower and weaponry he could get to rescue Elizabeth. He'd never been able to talk about his black ops days, and now probably wasn't the right time either. "Show me, and then I'll know."

His sons looked at each other, and he wished they weren't too big to turn over his knee because right now he'd love to whoop their asses.

"All right," Jesse grudgingly agreed. "But don't use it unless you absolutely have to."

"You're starting to sound like a broken record. You told me the same thing with the assault rifle."

That had been a chore getting one of those from his sons. It'd finally been Trent who'd walked up and handed him one, showing him how to use it, even though he knew the truth of Blake's secret black ops background.

He'd puffed out his chest every time he heard someone in government taut the strength of HIS. Hell, that was how he knew they'd succeed at rescuing

Elizabeth. They thought that his involvement could mess them up. He had to make sure that didn't happen.

The men, Kate, and Rylee suited up, and marched to the waiting SUVs Blake had acquired.

They were banking on it being Larry Thornton and him having Elizabeth in a home near Memphis, Tennessee. His heart pounded at the thought of it all. What if they were wrong? It'd been a big leap to choose Larry and then to select this home. There was no reason to believe Larry couldn't have taken her on a private flight except Devon assured them none had departed the Oxford or other nearby private airports.

If they were wrong, this would be a big hit to his career, but he pushed aside that thought. That potential hit would be worth it if they found Elizabeth or found a link to her.

His career didn't mean a thing to him if he didn't have Elizabeth by his side.

"Dad."

From the passenger seat, he turned to Jesse, who had driven. "Yeah?"

"We know what it's like to have a personal stake in things. We also know it can affect your judgment."

Blake didn't say anything as Jesse hadn't asked him a question. Yet. He knew it was coming.

"Are you sure you won't stand down and let us handle this? If nothing else, think of your career if this gets out."

"Fuck my career. When Kate was in trouble, did you stand down?"

The look of being gut-shot hit his son's eyes, and he knew he'd made his point. Blake heard the stories of when Kate and Jesse had been separated and she'd been in danger. AJ couldn't keep up with him as they'd raced to rescue her.

"No. It's just—" He cleared his throat. "It's just that you're not trained like we are."

His stomach lurched at the statement. He had to tell them. It was the only way to get them to relax. "It's probably time I shared something with you." He couldn't help that all of the men weren't in the vehicle, so Jesse gestured for him to use the comm system. He did. "Before I went into politics, I was in the military. Before I separated, I'd joined special ops, but I'd jumped into black ops."

Several "what the fucks" came back over the comm.

He ignored them and continued, "It wasn't for me and your mother, so I left at the end of my enlistment and sought a career in politics."

He cleared his throat. "I may be rusty as hell, but I understand what to expect. I want to be up-front and take down this fucker, but I'll leave it to you since you're current in your skills. I'll stay in the back. But when we find Elizabeth, I'm coming forward."

Jesse's nostrils flared as he inhaled. He'd always been a temperamental little shit. "Don't you think you could've told us sooner?"

"He told me," Trent piped up proudly.

"We have plenty of questions about this for you later. But until then, just don't accidentally shoot any of us in the back with that out-of-use trigger finger."

Chuckles drifted from his children, and he relaxed. He'd explain to them at some point, but there wasn't much more he could say that wasn't still classified. He'd breached part of it by telling Trent where he'd been on a mission that had gone horribly wrong. The last one he'd done for the Marines.

The drive seemed to take days even though it only took an hour or so. Dusk had settled before they left and during their drive, they were plunged into darkness with only a sliver of the moon to shine light on the back road they traveled. When they stopped about a quarter mile away from their destination, Blake recognized the area—courtesy of Google Earth.

"We'll find cover closer, but we wait until they're asleep," Jesse informed the vehicle occupants, even though they'd been told that before in their ops briefing. He turned to Blake. "Can you hold still that long?"

His heart pounded so loudly in his ears that he barely heard the question. "Yeah. I don't want to, but I understand why." He wanted to run in there and demand Larry release her, but since the bastards who'd entered his home had weapons, he had to assume all occupants would be armed. A shiver raced down his spine. She could get hurt if a miniwar erupted during her rescue.

They exited the vehicle and pride filled him with how his children had turned into warriors.

In the woods that were barely discernible since the little bit of light they had kept disappearing behind clouds that streamed by. Blake stayed close to Jesse. Not only because he'd promised, but because Jesse had a GPS tracker in his hand. The last thing Blake needed was to get lost and miss out on the entire thing, sending his sons and daughters-in-law to rescue him immediately after saving Elizabeth.

Jesse halted and Blake followed, his heart pounding a staccato rhythm against his chest. They must be close.

His eldest son put the GPS tracker in his pocket and slowly pulled his sniper rifle to his shoulder. Their goal was to get in at gunpoint, without a shot being fired, but if they couldn't even make it to the door, Jesse would be their hero of the hour.

Motioning Blake down, Jesse continued his sweep of the area through his scope, slowly, methodically.

Blake looked down and cringed. Lying down in the woods was not something he'd wanted to agree to. Ticks. Chiggers. Fleas. And not to mention snakes and other things he'd rather not have touch his body. But he had agreed, so he unhappily flattened himself on the ground. *God, I'm getting too old for this shit.*

Coldness seeped through the T-shirt he'd borrowed from Jesse. They'd had not only their weapons sent from Baltimore, but also their clothing, so everyone, including him, hid amongst the trees in camouflage pants and a black T-shirt. Ken, their team leader and organizer who put together their equipment, came up with a pair of combat boots in his size. Although a bit uncomfortable since they were new, he applauded his children's forward-thinking so he was best prepared—at least in the outfit department.

An ant crawled on his hand and bit. He slapped at it and bit back the sting from the bite. That little ant wrought a big-ass sting. He inwardly groaned. Yeah, he was definitely too old for this shit if an ant bite bothered him.

After what seemed like forever but had only been a couple of hours, Jesse motioned to Blake that they were ready to move.

His heart pounded mercilessly, and his palms were

sweaty. Not what he needed at the moment since he had a weapon to manage.

They stealthily crept through the woods, Blake's patience worn thin by how long it took. He didn't miss this. Never had. He'd convinced himself that he'd enlisted in the Marines as payback to Camilla's lie about being pregnant. He'd fought going into politics because that was what she'd wanted. When she'd decided having the military background would only make him a stronger candidate, his love of the Marines had died. Then, on that final mission, when he'd lost friends because their intel had been wrong....

Jesse held up a hand and stopped him. Then he held up two fingers. Two guards were patrolling. At least he hoped to hell that was what it meant.

In front of him, his son knelt and trained his weapon on something Blake couldn't see. The guards? Wasn't that the plan?

He needed to slap himself. Of course that was the plan. Not to kill them, but to be prepared in case they weren't friendly.

In his ear, he heard a soft "Go" from Jesse.

Every instinct in him wanted to do just that—go straight for Elizabeth, but he held his ground as some of the team surrounded the guards in an attempt to capture them instead of kill them. He knew that was best, but he wanted to rip them limb from limb for touching his Elizabeth.

If he hadn't been paying attention to Jesse because of the noise in his ear, he wouldn't have noticed his son get off a shot. The noise of the discharge had been low with the silencer—which he'd have to speak with Jesse about later. Weren't they illegal or something like that?

Even so, Jesse hadn't moved a muscle when he'd pulled the trigger, except to immediately train his weapon on a new spot.

A rush of emotion flooded him. Blake couldn't tell if he hit his target, but since he adjusted elsewhere, he assumed Jesse had. Yet that was it, his son had shot someone, maybe even killed them, and they weren't positive Elizabeth was here.

Over his comm, he learned one of the guards—the one Jesse had shot—hadn't wanted to play nice and confirmed Elizabeth was being held there. Relief at finding her and for his son's shot washed through his veins. The second guard—Blake heard in his ear—was willing to step aside—with some assistance from HIS— so Blake and company could enter the home. If he could be trusted, they knew not only the layout and where Elizabeth was being held but where Larry slept.

After securing both men—Jesse had only given the one guard an arm wound—they moved to the front and rear entrance of the home.

Blake's heart beat so loudly he couldn't hear anything in his earpiece over it. Hell, it pounded so hard he was surprised it was still in his chest. He wiped his palms on his pants and gripped his weapon, praying he wouldn't have to use it, before he fell in line behind his oldest son. That still seemed so ironic that the father had to follow the son into what could be a battle. Like any good parent, he wanted to protect his children, and part of him knew he couldn't be that rusty, that he could do it. But in this instance, he reluctantly agreed that the roles had to be reversed, or the consequences could be deadly.

On Jesse's count, they breached the house at the

same time—front and rear. Blake followed, urgency lacing into his system as he scanned the room for any threats. His mind was already on the staircase they were approaching.

Half of the team continued a sweep downstairs for any threats while the other half slowly made their way up the stairs, Blake in the rear wanting to shove them and make them go faster. At least they'd agreed he could go into the room to rescue Elizabeth. They probably figured there would be less of a threat there since Larry slept down the hallway.

A board creaked under AJ's feet and the team froze in place.

Chapter Thirteen

Elizabeth started at the creak of the board. All night she'd fretted over what might happen to her. Would Larry Thornton kill her now she knew who he was? Was he planning to come to her room and, heaven forbid, force himself on her?

Her blood rushed through her veins and her pulse raced, putting her limbs in fight or flight mode. But her mind stayed true to the fact that Blake would rescue her. Was that him?

Biting her lip in thought, she considered how she should handle the possible intruder coming up the stairs. Thinking back, Larry had already gone to bed, so it'd either be one of the guards or someone she hadn't met yet. Or Blake.

With no place to hide except a small closet which would be the first place someone looked, she decided to remain in the bathroom until she knew what kind of threat she had. If it was someone up to no good, she could rush them and hopefully get by them. If it was Blake, well…she'd probably rush him too, but only to be in his arms.

Silently she made her way to the bathroom. She grabbed the only thing that could be considered a weapon—the hairbrush. Then she put it back down. More than likely, she could do more damage with her hand and fist. Although that would hurt more. But if it helped her be free, she'd suffer it.

Then what? It was dark and she was lost. Her chest ached at the situation. She needed to escape, but she might be better off just waiting for rescue. Unless the person on the stairs meant her harm. She was driving herself insane mulling over the possibilities.

When the bedroom door slowly opened, she scooted back to only peek around the doorframe of the bathroom. Her breath caught in her throat, nearly choking her. Guns swept the room. She pulled herself back. How was she to overcome that? Closing her eyes, she fought back the tears misting her vision.

She was a survivor. She'd survived losing a husband and a daughter. She *would* survive this. No matter what.

Peeking back around, she saw a man standing in the doorway and someone pushing behind him. The man in the room had shown his face. Panic flashed through her. Were they here to kill her now since she knew who they were? Before, they'd worn weapons but had never carried them in this menacing manner.

Then she heard her name. Softly. Lovingly. *Blake.*

Without thought to the consequences, she rushed from the bathroom into the small bedroom, stopping near the man at the door as Blake pushed past him. She froze and her breath caught at the sight of Blake decked out in don't-fuck-with-me attire and carrying a gun—actually more than one gun. Sexy. Dangerous. God, she loved his man.

He slung his rifle over his shoulder and reached out to her. She fell into his arms and pulled herself tight against him.

Shouting from down the hallway reached her. It

sounded like Larry, but not only could she not make out what he was saying, she didn't care. She was safe. Blake had brought the army—or men who looked like they belonged in the army.

Unwinding his arms, he reached up with both hands and cradled her face. "God, Elizabeth. I'm so sorry." He touched his forehead to hers. "This is all my fault."

She put a finger to his lips. "Shh. It's not your fault. Larry told me everything. He was greedy and felt he was above it all. He told me that after it was over, no one could prove he kidnapped me, so he outed himself to me as a warning."

Dampness coated the corners of his eyes, and she wondered how much this tortured him. It truly wasn't his fault. Larry had tried to use Blake's position as chairman to sway the vote Larry's way. In fact—

She knew it wasn't the time, but her words spilled out anyway. "How did you know it was Larry Thornton? He said no one could ever tie him to the vote. He said he'd done things right to keep the pie bigger for him."

A smile played on his lips. "I can't wait to introduce you to my children. They're the reason we found you so quickly."

His lips touched hers lightly, as if he might break her by touching her harder, deeper. "I love you, Elizabeth."

This time, the smile was all hers. "I love you, too." Her lips covered his, and he immediately took over the kiss and almost took her breath away with the desperate need he demonstrated. And the heat. And the passion. So much passion resided in their locked lips that she was ready to strip him down right there in front of God knew who and have her way with him. She wanted him and that little thing he was doing with his tongue, to try to get her to open her lips, only added a cherry on top of everything.

Opening her mouth, his tongue swarmed in, demanding attention, and she wasn't one to deny him anything. Their tongues tangled while she wound her arms around him and tried to pull herself closer, to feel his body up against hers.

A firestorm built inside her and she knew they had to stop before she really did start peeling off his clothes. Heat flooded her cheeks at the thought of them getting caught having sex. She had to be the one to call a halt because he didn't seem to care who was around since he'd rubbed his arousal against her.

Cognizant of the noise around them, she sighed and slowly separated them.

Blake tried to pull her back, but she shook her head and mouthed, "People." As if he'd just noticed them, he snapped out of his haze and looked around the room that had seen its visitors decrease to one other.

"Dad," the man who had entered with Blake said.

Putting his arm around her, Blake pulled Elizabeth to his side.

"Elizabeth, this is my eldest son, Jesse." Pride filled his voice, the type of pride that only comes from a parent.

"It's nice to meet you." Jesse stuck out a hand to her.

Stunned that this big man who looked like he'd rip someone's head off was Blake's son, she could only nod as she shook his large hand.

He turned to Blake. "Give me your weapons, Dad," Jesse insisted.

"What?" Blake asked.

"Give me your weapons. No one needs to see that you were carrying during this."

"What's the matter?"

"Your career. This one is for your career. We're calling the police, and we don't need Larry or one of his guards telling them you're carrying without a permit."

"You don't have a permit in Mississippi, or wait… Tennessee." He tilted his head. "Do you?"

Jesse smiled, his teeth gleaming in the light. "Trust me, Dad." He held out his hand, and Blake handed him his rifle, a handgun from his waistband, and something that looked like a grenade.

Her eyes snapped to Blake's and she saw his hand-caught-in-a-candy-jar grin. And she loved it.

Chapter Fourteen

It was a few hours before they trudged into the Oxford home. Dealing with the police had taken longer than they'd hoped. A Mississippi senator on Tennessee grounds where a shooting occurred had the local law enforcement officers' chops salivating. Blake expected it'd be in the news since he had no one who'd been available to control the story. He'd woken Randy up in the middle of the night to get a press release put together, even though that meant waking other staff members.

While he was at it, he had his staff draw up another press release to be ready for when Elizabeth said yes to marrying him. He could barely wait to tell the world that she was his—his forever.

First, he had to allow her to recuperate from the ordeal she'd just endured. From all accounts, she'd been treated well, but she'd still been woken in the night and kidnapped with no idea what would happen to her. It had to have been frightening beyond measure.

"I'm hungry," AJ said as they shuffled through the front door. "Think Mary's up?"

His youngest son could eat twenty-four hours a day if allowed. How AJ had never been as big as a house baffled him. Walking through the portal with Elizabeth's hand in his, he shook his head. "No, but we can whip something up ourselves. I taught all of you boys how to cook."

Several groans sounded as they all continued toward the kitchen.

"Don't tell me that being married has turned you into some kind of useless twits now, unable to care for yourselves."

Kate laughed. "Believe me, Jesse is far from that."

"Ditto," Rylee added with a sly smile to Devon.

Stopping inside the big country kitchen, he dropped Elizabeth's hand and moved to his two present daughters-in-law. Putting a hand on each of their shoulders, he smiled. "Have I told you how glad I am you joined our family? Not just for today, but for every day you make my sons happy."

Rylee blinked fast as if staving off tears.

Kate spoke up, "I'm sure I speak for Rylee, but we're glad to be part of your family. We're in love with our husbands and we love you and your other sons."

This time he blinked rapidly. These women had a way to move his heart with love. His family had never been so lucky. Now, if only Matt and Brad would find their special someone.

"Okay, get those weapons put away so the little ones won't be tripping over them," he directed. "Two of you stay in here with me to cook."

As if she'd expected them to be awake so early, Mary shuffled into the kitchen and began shooing everyone out of the way so she could cook breakfast for not only them but his other daughters-in-law that she said would be down as soon as all of the children were cared for.

It appeared no one slept, or slept much, during their daring rescue.

Sitting at the table by themselves while the others disposed of their weapons, Blake held Elizabeth's hand in his own, lacing his fingers in hers. "I know I've asked a ton, but how are you, really?"

A warm smile spread across her face. Sunshine. It reminded him of sunshine. How could she smile so after everything? This was one hell of a woman. "Really, Blake. I'm fine. Tired, but fine. They didn't hurt me. Only frightened me. But now I wonder if they actually meant it." She shrugged her shoulders lazily. "It doesn't matter. Larry was caught red-handed, so to speak, so it's over." Her eyes widened. "What about your career? I really think that one beefy cop was going to blab it to the press. He seemed eager to get you to do or say something newsworthy. Not that your being there wasn't already newsworthy."

Chuckling, he slowly shook his head. "Randy's got the team on it. It's okay. I was there rescuing you, so I can't see how anyone can get anything bad from that. I have to hand it to my eldest son, though. That was a stroke of genius taking everything away from me. Going in after you, defenseless....Hell, they might make me a hero for that." He winked at her.

Laughter bubbled up from her. Beautiful laughter. Thank God she didn't have any lasting effects from her brief kidnapping.

How the hell did he get so lucky?

The group trudged back into the kitchen, a couple of extra daughters-in-law and grandchildren in the mix. He hadn't understood when Camilla had wanted the huge bench table in their kitchen back then. Now, he saw she'd been forward planning to days like this. He hoped she looked down at her children and smiled at all they'd accomplished and their new families.

"Here, Dad." AJ handed a squirming Alex to him. "He wants his Poppy."

Blake chuckled at how they continued teaching the kids Poppy after his first granddaughter had called him that and no one had challenged her on it. It'd stuck, and now his children were teaching their children to call him that. It was damn endearing, and he wanted to give them all a bear hug for it.

With a few seated at the bar, everyone else found a seat at the table, albeit a little snug, but no one complained. He'd have to have an extension added on for the more daughters-in-law he expected and grandchildren. Maybe he'd find a place to build a children's table. Then again, he had to leave that to Emily and Jake to decide.

It occurred to him that while he'd introduced Elizabeth to his family at Larry's house while waiting for the police, she hadn't met everyone else. So he introduced her to Emily, Megan, Kelly, Jason—his adopted teenage grandson—and the little ones. All who'd stayed behind.

Mary set two carafes of coffee on the table and then returned with a tray of mugs. She emptied the tray and returned with more mugs plus sugar, that nonsugar stuff, and creamer. God Bless the woman.

"How did you and Dad meet?" Emily asked as she handed around mugs.

Elizabeth glanced at him questioningly.

He motioned his head for her to answer. He wouldn't do all of the communication. Elizabeth was strong, and he wanted the family to get to know her.

"We met at a fundraiser."

"Tux and all, Dad?" Emily joked.

Blake chuckled. "No, just suit. But Elizabeth was running it and took my breath away."

Matt poured coffee for himself. "What fundraiser this time, Dad?"

Hesitating, he looked at Elizabeth to prepare her. "Diamond Blackfan Anemia Awareness."

"I've never heard of it," Megan said, swishing back and forth two pink bags of sugar substitute.

"It only affects a small part of the population, but it can be deadly."

A moment of silence reigned as if paying homage to all the victims of the disease.

"Why that one, Elizabeth?" Devon asked before taking a sip of coffee.

Knowing she needed the comfort, and wanting to give it to her, he shifted Alex to his other arm and held her hand, giving it a gentle squeeze.

"I— I lost my only daughter to it."

This time the silence hung heavy. It was one thing to hear about a deadly disease, but to meet someone who lost a child to it—unimaginable.

"I'm sorry," came from several of the people at the table, and he was proud he'd taught them respect and they'd found wives and a husband with the same etiquette.

Mary arrived to save the day with a stack of plates, then returned with silverware. After that, platters of eggs, bacon, sausage, grits, and biscuits hit the table, and the family dug in like they'd been starved.

Megan took Alex from him and set him up in the high chair that Blake had stored for when the kids visited. Looked like they'd need to get another one since he'd have two at the same time within that high chair age range.

The plates were nearly clean before conversation returned to the group.

"What ended up happening tonight?" Megan leaned forward and looked down the table at Elizabeth. "I'm glad they rescued you."

Beside her, AJ shrugged. "Nothing happened."

Brad scoffed. "Except Jesse shooting someone."

Elizabeth's hand flew to her mouth, and she turned to Blake. "Someone got shot?"

"He needed it." AJ shrugged and reached for another biscuit. "Besides, it wasn't a mortal wound. The guy wouldn't stand down." He turned to his wife and almost pleaded with her to understand. "He planned to shoot us, and Jesse kept that from happening. It's what he does as a sniper."

"Oh." Megan appeared taken aback.

Waving his butter knife at her, AJ said, "You'd have to be there to understand."

Her eyes narrowed into tiny slits. "AJ Hamilton, have you forgotten how we met? What I learned went on? I just meant I'd hoped it'd been civil, for Elizabeth's sake."

"Oh." AJ nodded amid snickers from the family.

With a smile of his own, Blake couldn't say it enough—*God, he loved his family*.

Chapter Fifteen

Without hesitation or doubt, Elizabeth loved Blake's family—both sides of it. The big, menacing group rescuing her, and the fun, loving group having breakfast together. By all appearances, they seemed to accept her.

She wasn't sure she'd thanked them enough. Wasn't sure she could thank them enough. It might have been easy to breach the place and rescue her, but things might not have been, yet they went in anyway. For her. Because Blake was their father.

And Blake, standing there with a rifle and other weaponry, had her heart still racing in excitement. He'd looked fierce, yet sexy as all get out. She should've taken a picture before they removed his weapons if for nothing else than the memory of her savior...her hero. She couldn't imagine many people would've gone to the depths of getting their family involved in such a feat. No, some would've called the police and made things worse, others would've done whatever was asked, but Blake...Blake proved he would do anything necessary to protect those he loves, and she was mighty glad that included her.

In the shower, she washed away any feeling of being held hostage, of meeting the slimeball Larry Thornton. Of being near his men, all masked to preserve their identities. She laughed. They never expected Blake to turn the tables, or they'd have been better prepared.

She was still in awe that Jesse had shot one of the men because he'd been prepared to harm them. She'd never wanted anyone harmed trying to save her, but if someone had been, she was glad it had been the bad guys and not her knights—and princesses—in shining armor. Well, fatigues. Same principle.

She opened the shower door and jerked back in surprise. Her hands flew to her breasts reflexively, even knowing she didn't need to hide. "Blake."

With a cocky grin, he held out a fluffy towel. "Let me dry you off." His tone held more of a command than an offering in it.

She almost argued that she could do it, but the thought of his hands on her sent a delicious shiver racing up her spine.

When she hesitated, he drew her attention to his crotch and the monster hard-on stuffed in his pants.

"See what you do to me?" Heat burned in his eyes, but she liked the fire in his playfulness just as much. "At my age, I should be looking at little blue pills, but when I'm around you, I'm like this all the freakin' time."

Stunned at the frequency he wanted her, her own arousal licked at her with a heat and need so strong she fought grabbing for him and racing to the bedroom. But having him dry her off could be enough foreplay to send her on an erotic spin. Yeah, she wanted it. With a mischievous smile, she opened her arms like she had before the kidnapping, stretching them out to the sides so he knew she was ready for him to go to work. He seemed to love her in this pose.

He rubbed the soft cloth lightly on her calves and feet. Lifting each foot, he took special care to dry every toe and kissed the top of her foot before he replaced it on the floor.

Her breath caught when he dried her inner thighs, briefly touching her core, just enough to tease her. His knowing smile acknowledged that fact. She'd remember this when it was her turn to touch him.

When he reached her breasts, goosebumps spread across her skin. A firestorm of heat touched her every nerve ending, leaving her burning with need for him to be inside her. "Hurry," she pleaded.

Instead, he took a puckered nipple in his mouth, suckled on it, then, with his tongue, laved the area around it in slow, sensual circles, driving her insane with lust.

The towel all but forgotten, he tended to her other breast with as much passion as he'd given the first one. With a nip on the rigid peak, she gasped and tossed her head back at the pleasure driving through her system.

With a hand behind her neck, he tilted her head back to him until they were face-to-face, their lips almost touching, their warm breaths mingling.

Then his lips took hers in a demanding, punishing kiss that easily bruised. Heat then flared at her core when his tongue intruded into her mouth, pursuing dominance. He'd never exerted this much of a forcible presence in their lovemaking.

She liked it.

A lot.

As their tongues intertwined, the kiss shifted, and the punishing part disappeared as a tenderness seeped into their lips.

He wrapped his arms around her and pulled her tight.

He broke the kiss. "I can never get enough of you," he whispered hoarsely, his forehead resting against hers.

Pulling her closer, her breasts pushed into his chest, her hard nipples rubbing against the firmness of his body.

"I can't get enough of you, either. Take me to bed."

He did something unprecedented. Treating her as if she weighed less than a rag doll, he swung her into his arms and marched them to the bedroom. With all gentleness, he deposited her on the bed and impatiently divested himself of his clothing.

She'd never tire of seeing his magnificent body, all lean lines and tone. His hard cock stood up with need for her.

Scooting back, she lay down and made room for him. She patted the bedsheets beside her. "Come here," she demanded in a soft, firm voice. She inwardly smirked. It was her turn to play.

With a wicked grin, he crawled onto the bed and plopped down in the spot she designated. He leaned over the top of her and took her mouth again. This time devouring it with such hunger she was almost floored by the strength of it.

Moving, she maneuvered them over to where she rested on top of him. She broke the heavy kiss and moaned at the loss of his lips, but she had work to do. "You're always making love to me. It's my turn to make love to you." With the exception of their one time together here, he always went down on her and prepped her for their lovemaking, typically giving her two orgasms each time with each bout of sex. The man knew his way around her body.

Sliding down him, she pressed soft kisses to his chest, twirling the curly hair in her fingers as she glided her hand down his hard chest.

When she reached his navel, she ran her tongue in a circle around it and almost giggled when he inhaled deeply and sucked his stomach in as far as he could while pressed into the bed.

His hand, which had rested on her head, gently pushed the hair from her face so he could see her actions and reactions.

She smiled at him, then followed the thin path of hair that led to his cock. When she grasped it lightly, he tensed, making her smile even more. She worked her hand, stroking up and down, teasing him as she did.

As she neared his cock with her mouth, he groaned. The sound drove her forward, reverberating against her core, spiking up her own heat level.

She licked him from the base to the tip of his rigidness, then licked a circle around the head, swooping in to taste the precum that had appeared during her ministrations.

"You're killing me," he rasped.

"Oh, so you want me to stop?" she teased.

"Hell, no. I want to be balls deep in your sweet mouth."

"I'll just have to comply then since you said it so pleasantly." She giggled and opened her mouth to take his cock inside, letting it slide down her throat as deep as possible.

"Good God."

Sucking and licking her way up and down his

shaft, while her hands helped in the process, her own desire grew, and her wetness increased. She teased the tender centerline along the base of his cock with her tongue and cupped his balls, massaging.

She wanted to fuck him something fierce, but she promised him this.

He grabbed her and yanked her up and onto her back in the gentlest way possible, yet it startled her until he hovered over her, settling between her thighs. His male hardness touched her heated core, and she wanted to fly with ecstasy.

"I have to have you, Elizabeth."

"Then have me, Blake."

Without further ado, he shoved his cock forward and deep into her pussy. She gasped and quivered around him. Then she moaned at the fullness, the rightness of it all.

After planting a kiss at the tender spot below her earlobe, he made his way with wet, hot kisses down her neck. "I love you," he rasped as he moved his hips, sliding in and out of her, driving her mad with pleasure.

"I love you, too." She lifted her legs and wrapped them around her waist, smiling when he groaned.

He withdrew and surged forward again. She thrust her hips to drive him deeper and deeper until she gave up all hopes of controlling their sweet lovemaking.

"I want you hard and fast. Show me how much you want me," she whispered.

He groaned. "I wanted to go slow and love every inch of you."

"You can do that later tonight. Show me how much you really want me right now."

He appeared to war with himself before he drove

into her with a force to be reckoned with.

She smiled and held on as he pounded into her, touching her very soul with need until she began that climb. Not wanting to be alone, she whispered, "I'm close. Are you close?"

"I've been ready to explode for a while now. I want you to come first."

"Together," she said in a silent demand and plea all in one.

He clenched his jaw. "Together."

Keeping his strokes firm, he drove her up that cliff until she splintered, starbursts forming before her eyes, and she fell into a pillow of pleasure so soft and warm she didn't want to let it go to come back to reality.

So lost in her orgasm that she barely registered when Blake spilled himself in her with a grunt of satisfaction.

Lifting himself off her body, and sliding beside her, he sighed heavily. "God, you're going to kill me."

A smile split her face. "But it's the good kind, isn't it?"

"I'll never give you up."

That meant he definitely saw a future for them. Her heart soared to new heights.

They were quiet for a few minutes before she spoke, hesitantly. "Does that mean we can go public with our relationship?"

Fretful that she'd pushed too far when he didn't answer right away, she glanced over at him, only to find him sound asleep, with a smile on his face.

Chapter Sixteen

Blake woke refreshed and ready to do all he had to accomplish today. First, he had something important to do, and he wouldn't put it off any longer. Sure, he'd promised Camilla he'd wait, but he'd been breaking a lot of promises he'd made that he thought were wrong for the people involved. He'd told Trent, and while that hadn't turned out as he'd expected—hell, he hadn't known what to expect—he was glad it was out in the open. It was time to announce it to the world.

There was absolutely no reason to wait. It was just a controlling thing his late wife had put in place. He was done with her bonds. He would set this right.

In the living room, most of his children were lounging around the couch and many chairs, staring at a cartoon on the television with cups of coffee in their hands. He shook his head. Children had a way of changing what parents watched.

Continuing in the room, he bypassed his grandchildren sprawled on the floor, eyes glued to the television, and walked to Emily who was seated on one of the couches. "Hold out your hand."

With furrowed brows, she hesitantly followed his dictate.

Opening his hand over hers, he dropped the folded documents in his hand to hers.

For a moment she stared at him, then reached over

and unfolded them, slowly as if they were antiquated and could fall apart at her touch. When she read the document title, she gasped so loudly that Jake, who'd been sitting next to her, surged forward to check on her.

Blake smiled when she looked up at him with bewilderment. "Your mother wanted you to have the house. She said on your twenty-fifth birthday, but I think it's okay to do it now." Two years early wouldn't kill anything. Emily was mature enough to handle the responsibility.

"Are you sure, Dad?" Her hands trembled around the documents, and her eyes glistened with tears. He hoped for happy tears.

"All I ask is that this remains a place for the family. There's a trust set up for the maintenance of the house and to keep Mary and Henry on board and then retire them when they're ready." He wouldn't add that since the employees had come later, there'd been no stipulation for them in the initial trust. He'd added that part because he never wanted Emily to have to make that difficult financial choice.

His daughter had always been bright and processed things quickly, which was probably why she'd picked up numbers so fast and had become a highly skilled forensic accountant. "But if we change this from the dummy corporation you have set up"—one he'd created to protect his and his family's privacy—"then we can't use this as a safe house any longer. People will be able to find it."

Before he could speak, Jesse was standing beside him. "Em, we won't use this as a safe house any longer. We have one we don't use often enough. It needs to start earning its keep. Change the ownership. I remember mom talking about this house and how she wanted to pass it to her daughter before you were even born."

"But what about the rest of you?" Guilt lanced her expression. "It should be for everyone, not just me."

Blake shook his head. "No," he said adamantly. "This house has been passed down to firstborn daughters of the family. You need to pass it down to Amber if you want to keep with a very long tradition. I think a long lost relative of yours wanted to ensure the women of the family didn't have to have a man."

Emily smiled at that, as brightly as the sun. She stood and flung her arms around him. "Thank you, Dad." Wet drops hit his chest as she wept with happiness. He imagined having something from her mother meant the world to her, which was another reason he wanted to do it now. She deserved to know that her mother loved her since she'd lost her when she was two years old and didn't have the memories of motherly hugs and loving acts like kissing wounds.

It'd been a long time since he'd really held his daughter. Visions of her as a child crying over an injury or what she felt was a slight from her brothers flooded him, and his emotions choked him up. Love welled inside him enough that it made his eyes watery. He would not cry at this moment. He would be strong for his daughter who deserved the world handed to her.

Emily pulled back and wiped her cheeks with the backs of her hands. "Thank you," she whispered.

Jake, who'd stood beside her when she'd jumped to her feet, shook his hand. "Thank you," he echoed.

A chorus of congratulations came from his other children. The men had all known before that Emily would get the house. Blake had explained the tradition. None had balked at it or called it an injustice. He figured they were glad she'd have something so that she'd always be taken care of, because no matter the grief they gave her growing up, they loved and adored their baby sister.

After everything had settled down, he looked back up the stairs, made sure they were empty, then cleared his throat. "It's time for me to do what I told you that I was doing. Tonight, I'm asking Elizabeth to marry me. I want your help."

"Sure, Dad. Anything you need. We like Elizabeth," Matt said.

Agreement echoed through the group.

He released a heavily burdened sigh and relief flowed through him. He'd needed to know that they really cared for her, and this strong show of support—before they even knew what he asked—overwhelmed him. If that was even possible.

"Here's what I'd like," he started.

Chapter Seventeen

The wind had picked up, making the evening chilly. Elizabeth pulled the wrap closer around her shoulders, enjoying the company of the Hamilton family during a cookout. Blake could grill a good steak, that was for sure. Whenever she didn't feel like cooking, she'd set him to the grill. Of course, she wasn't sure how his housekeeper slash cook would feel about Elizabeth taking over the kitchen.

First things first. One of them had to propose. As much as she wanted to, she wasn't brave enough to do it with all of his children present. That was too much pressure. Maybe he wasn't truly ready for them to come out in the open. He was so hard to read.

Of course, their story would leak, and it'd be known he was involved—somehow—in her rescue. There was no way he could keep that quiet. How would he handle it?

She was ready for them to come out of the closet—so to speak. She deserved to have a regular romantic relationship with a man. And that man was Blake Hamilton. Now, how to get him to move to that next level....

Either once the kids left, or she and Blake did, if he hadn't asked her to marry him, she would propose. But when they were alone, just in case she was humiliated. But he loved her, so it should be good. That was what she kept telling herself—he loved her. It'd work out.

Startled by movement, she looked up, and Emily stepped forward and offered her a rose. Elizabeth held her shawl with one hand and accepted the peach rose with the other. "You're an incredible woman," Blake's daughter told her. She turned and walked away.

Next, Jake approached. Before he could reach out, she dropped the shawl so she could have both hands. He also handed her a rose. Thank goodness they'd removed the thorns. Before he could speak, she peeked around him and noticed all Blake's children had lined up with a rose in their hands. Tears welled in her eyes at the loving gesture. She was so overwhelmed that she missed what Jake said to her. She was too embarrassed to ask him to repeat it. He didn't seem to expect a reply as he walked away and Matt walked to her.

Handing her a rose, Matt flashed a brilliant smile. "It's an honor to know you." Knowing he'd been a Navy SEAL, expanded her heart, and the tears brimmed her eyelids, trying to break free.

He departed, and his twin approached. He offered her his rose and added his somewhat cocky smile. "We hope you choose us," Brad said, confusing her with his statement.

Devon, with his little smirk, took his turn. "Just in the little time we've known you, I can see why Dad loves you."

She fought the tears from leaking down her face, but it was so damn hard. These men, and women, touched her heart, and she still had one more to go. When Devon leaned over and kissed her cheek, she lost the battle, a tear slipped down, gliding slowly until it dropped off in her lap.

By the time Jesse stepped up, she was freely crying, albeit silently. Her heart had warmed so much by this little act of acceptance.

Jesse handed her his rose. "Dad has something to ask you, and we hope you say yes."

Her breath caught, and her heart did a pitter-patter. Did he mean what she thought? Was Blake really going to propose to her?

When Jesse departed with a sly grin on his face, Blake took his place.

"I want to do this right, but you may have to help me up." He grinned cheekily.

She gasped even though she'd already guessed what he was doing. His telling her just made it real. And he was doing it in front of his children. The children who had just told her—in their own way—they wanted her to be part of their family. She swiped at the tears with her fingers and wiped them on the discarded shawl in her lap.

Down on one knee, Blake opened a blue jeweler's box with a gorgeous princess-cut diamond in it. One that was way too big in her mind. Then again, could a diamond ring ever be too big? She only needed something small, but she'd take whatever he gave her because *he* gave it to her.

"Elizabeth Page, you are pure sunshine on my rainy days. You are the brightest stars on my darkest days. With you, my life is full of love, compassion, and joy. I need you in my life. Please say you'll marry me and be my wife. My partner for the rest of our lives."

Her heart was nearly exploding from the love infused in it. Ignoring the tears, she scooted off the chair, and dropped to her knees in front of him.

He looked at her surprised and with a bit of fear in his gaze. Had he thought she'd say anything but yes?

"Yes. Yes, I'll marry you," she breathed as she leaned forward and pressed her lips to his. Fire exploded in her body, but she ignored it and pulled back. "I love you, Blake Hamilton."

"I love you." His shaking hand removed the ring from the box.

She shoved the roses in her right hand and held out her left one for him. Hers shook also but not nearly as bad as his.

The man had truly been nervous about proposing to her.

Blake had done well. The ring was only about a half-size too big. She could fix that when they were home. She wanted to squeal like a schoolgirl. Soon, home would be with him.

He kissed her again, and she heard clapping from their audience, whom she'd forgotten.

They rose and accepted the congratulations of the Hamilton children and spouses.

"When are you going to get married?" someone asked.

Blake looked at her. "As soon as she'll agree."

"Is tomorrow soon enough," she joked.

A wicked smile crossed his face. "I'd hoped you would say that. I have someone all lined up."

She didn't know whether to be upset or overjoyed, so she went with the happier emotion. She didn't need fancy. She just needed Blake in her life. Forever.

Chapter Eighteen

"Dad, you seem awfully nervous. Are you sure you want to do this?" AJ asked.

Blake turned from his spot, adjusting his tie in the mirror, and glanced at his sons with a critical eye. He'd been blessed to have them and for them to grow up as they had. They'd become true gentlemen, and he couldn't be prouder of them or the lives they'd chosen. But that didn't mean he didn't want to chuck something at his son's head for saying that.

They'd gone through this when he'd spoken with them before he'd asked Elizabeth to marry him. There was no way in hell he would back out. He loved the woman with everything inside him. As corny as the saying was, he hadn't felt complete before her. Oh, his children completed him in the paternal aspect, but in sharing a life with someone....

He narrowed his eyes at AJ. "I remember someone who paced the room at about ninety miles an hour while he was waiting to get married."

The room erupted in laughter and his apparent nerves were forgotten. Or so he'd thought.

"You know, Dad, you can still call it off if you're not sure," Matt said.

"I'll remember you said that when it's your turn." *Shit.* He immediately felt contrite when Matt's face fell. Matt had been engaged to Caitlyn in college until the unthinkable happened, and she'd left without a word. "I'm sorry."

"It's no big deal."

Being the father he was, he decided to allow that lie to slide because it had been one hell of a big deal to Matt at the time, and he was sure it still was because he remained single. Then again, so was his twin.

"Boys," he said over a lump in his throat. "I know I've already said it, but thank you for your help in rescuing Elizabeth. Your mother was special to me"—they didn't need to know the specifics—"but Elizabeth is my world now. My heart would've stopped without her."

Jesse leaned off the door and strode to him. He reached up and straightened Blake's tie. "We're happy for you. You've been alone too long."

Around his son, he saw nods throughout the group sprawled on the bed or leaning against the walls, all dressed in the best they'd brought for the trip. All seven of them—Jake and Trent included—would stand up for him today, and he didn't care that they didn't match or that they all weren't wearing sports coats. They were his sons, and they were here with him at one of the most monumental times of his life—their births being first.

A knock sounded at the door. "Pastor Gary is here."

True nerves skittered along his spine. While there was nothing to be nervous about, it didn't stop the feeling. Maybe he'd misinterpreted and it was anxiety. He liked that better because he couldn't marry her fast enough.

Thank goodness the church had agreed to marry

them without the prolonged counseling they generally required. Elizabeth wanted to be married by the church and he wanted to be married as quickly as possible, so they'd passed the test and were able to expedite their wedding.

The flower garden on the grounds of the Oxford home had been their choice. Elizabeth had made sure to ask Emily's permission to use it. She'd also offered to move them out of the master bedroom, but his daughter had stated that the bedroom belonged to her father and his wife.

How had he gotten so lucky with her too? Especially when his boys were such hellions growing up, and she'd tried to follow them everywhere. Thank goodness for Trent, as he'd kept her out of trouble.

Outside, he ran his finger between his collar and neck, feeling constricted. He'd brought and worn his favorite gray suit—the one he'd worn when he met her—and a gray and burgundy tie to wear in case she'd said yes, and they could marry right away. In preparing for the trip, he'd told her to bring a dressy outfit, or he'd feared she'd have had to have a shopping trip before they tied the knot.

It'd been bad enough he'd had to wait for her best friend, Crystal, to fly in as her maid of honor. It'd touched his heart when she'd asked his daughter and daughters-in-law to also stand up with her. After a brief discussion about the children, Amber and Reagan were selected as flower girls. Megan and Kelly thanked Elizabeth for the offer but volunteered to sit and take care of Ashley, Alexander, and the girls during the ceremony because, at this point, their only attendees were Jason, Mary, and Henry. Everyone else was in the ceremony.

He shook his head at the absurdity of it. Yet he wouldn't have picked one of his sons over the other for the honor of being best man. They did play rock-paper-scissors—several times actually—to see who would sign the marriage license as a witness though. AJ won, which wasn't a surprise since he always won when the boys competed against each other. Had they rigged this too? Not that it mattered.

The pastor motioned to Megan, who doubled as their music coordinator. She pressed a button and music played through two speakers they'd set up near the arbor. The men and the pastor awaited Elizabeth.

First, Kate walked toward him, smiling brightly, although he wasn't sure if the smile was for him or Jesse, who stood right beside him. Rylee strode toward him, her hands wrapped around the stems of fresh picks from the flower garden. When his little girl started her trek toward him, his gaze misted at her happiness for him. Yeah, she looked straight at him, not her husband.

Crystal came next, and while Blake had never really warmed to her, he didn't dislike her, except she'd tried to convince Elizabeth she needed a shopping day and a separate spa day before this could happen. That was after it'd taken her two days to arrive.

Reagan and Amber came toward him in cute little dresses and baskets Mary had found that she'd filled with rose petals. His heart almost burst with love. Reagan was meticulous in dropping them in a line while Amber dropped handfuls at a time wherever they landed.

When the girls approached them, he knelt—knees cracking and all—and kissed each on the cheek before sending them over to Megan.

Not that he didn't love seeing everyone else, but he wanted to see his future wife. He could hardly wait until he dropped the term future from it.

Megan made an adjustment with the music and everyone refocused their gaze to the back of the house. His breath caught at the vision gliding toward them. In a light blue dress and wearing her hair pulled up with flowers woven into the tresses, this woman knocked his socks off all over again with her beauty and grace. His love for her knew no bounds.

Walking toward her, to the gasps of the women and chuckles of the men, he met her halfway down their makeshift aisle and stopped. They stared at each other for a moment. "You're beautiful," he breathed.

Her smile lit her face. "Thank you."

As if suddenly realizing himself, he stepped beside her, turned around toward the laughing crowd and offered his arm. "How about we get married?"

A Note From Sheila

Thank you for reading *His Family*! If you enjoyed reading Blake and Elizabeth's story, I would appreciate it if you would help others enjoy this book, too. You can do that by recommending it to friends, readers' groups, and discussion boards. It would mean a great deal to me if you'd take a moment to write a review and share how you feel about my story so others may find my work. Honest reviews help bring my books to the attention of other readers. The best news, only a few words are needed.

A word about the author...

Sheila Kell writes about romantic men who leave women's hearts pounding with a happily ever after built on memorable, adrenaline-pumping stories. Her debut novel, *His Desire* (HIS Series #1), launched as an Amazon #1 romantic suspense bestseller, later winning the Readers' Favorite award for best romantic suspense novel.

As a Southern girl who has left behind her days with the United States Air Force and as a University Vice President, she can usually be found on the Mississippi coast, where she lives with her cats and all the strays that magically find her front door. When she isn't writing, you can find Sheila with her nose in a good book, dealing with the woodland critters who enjoy her back porch, or wishing she had a genie to do her bidding.

Ways to connect

SheilaKell.com

facebook.com/sheilakellbooks

goodreads.com/sheilakellbooks

bookbub.com/authors/sheila-kell

I'd love to hear directly from you, too. Please feel free to email me at sheila@sheilakell.com.

Don't miss out on new releases, exclusive excerpts, and giveaways!

Join my newsletter:

www.SheilaKell.com/subscribe